CONSTRUCTION AND CALAMITY

JULIA KOTY

BUSSTOP PRESS

First paperback edition June 2021

Cover design by Kim Thurlow
Book design by Natasha Sass

ISBN 978-1-939309-09-9 (paperback)
ISBN 978-1-939309-10-5 (large print paperback)
ISBN 978-1- 939309-08-2(ebook)
www.JuliaKoty.com

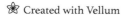

To Daddy who renovated the old victorian that appears in this story
and
To Mommy who cooked every single day in that kitchen
I love you both.

ALSO BY JULIA KOTY

1

I climbed around another pile of junk. The spring had been cool, but a warm May breeze floated across the hodge-podge of miscellaneous stuff. It didn't quite smell like the dumpster behind the diner, but it was close. The recycling center could use a bit more organization. And that's saying a lot coming from a person who hates organizing. "I can't believe you talked me into this," I complained.

Aerie flipped back her blond ponytail. "We'll find stuff for your kitchen, Mira, I just know it."

I had been unlucky enough that my kitchen had burned down soon after arriving in town. Aerie has helped me ever since. "Can you know it faster? I'm not a fan of dumpster diving."

"We're not in the dumpsters, just near them. Oh, look a cutting board."

"I could never clean that enough to make me want to use it."

Aerie shrugged and placed it gently on the pile.

I walked toward the back of the lean-to. She was

technically right; we were only *near* the dumpsters not in them. The town had decided to set up a freecycle center near the recycle dumpsters in town. Complete with its own roof. But underneath this roof were piles of junk. Still, Aerie was sure we'd find a diamond in the rough for my kitchen.

"You never know what people throw out. Maybe there's a mixer here, or a blender."

I nodded. I doubted it though. Until I noticed something. Metallic red shined back at me from around the end of the row of junk. What could that be? Moving away a grey trash bag of, I hoped, clothes, I saw what had caught my eye. Surrounded by beat-up random items on the black asphalt sat a shiny red and white popcorn maker. It looked like it could be from a state fair or something. And brand new, too. "Hey Aerie, look what I found."

Excited she ran over. "Oh, my goodness, that's awesome." She shook my arm. "See, I told you we'd find something."

"I can't use this in my kitchen. It's huge." The popcorn machine was practically 3 feet tall *and* wide.

"But look at it! It looks brand new."

"If it's here then it probably doesn't work."

"Maybe." Aerie shrugged, acknowledging what was obvious to me. "We should take it back to the diner to see if we can get it to work. If you don't want it..."

I held my hands up. "It's way too big for my kitchen and I don't even like popcorn."

"What?" She stopped her trash removal and stared at me. "How do I not know this?" We'd become pretty close friends over the last few months.

"I only like movie theater popcorn," I informed her.

"But this looks like we could make some authentic

movie theater popcorn with this shiny baby. Are you sure you don't want it?"

I laughed. "I'm sure. I'll help you load it in the back of the car."

Surprisingly the popcorn machine wasn't as heavy as it appeared. More awkward than anything. But getting it into the trunk of Babs, my ancient Buick, proved to be a comedy of errors. We almost dropped the thing twice. I couldn't even slightly close the trunk. "I'd feel better if the trunk were down so I could see out the rear window and we'd know this thing wasn't about to jump ship."

After a few moments Aerie wandered back into the pile of junk. "These will work." She held up a pair of dirty bungee cords.

"Sorry Babs," I apologized to my longtime clunker. I felt bad for subjecting her to the nasty bungee cords hooked up under her trunk.

But the cords managed to hold the trunk lid down and we drove back to the diner. When we got back Aerie was bent on clearing space next to the milkshake machine.

"Hold up. Let me at least wipe this thing down before we put it up on the counter where actual food is handled."

"You're right." Aerie and I headed to the kitchen where we each grabbed a sponge, and I grabbed the bottle of diluted bleach that I used to clean the countertops. After spraying and wiping it down, the practically new popcorn machine gleamed.

Aerie bounced on her toes in excitement. "We can put it right next to the milkshake machine. It will look perfect."

I had to admit it looked like it belonged. "We don't even know if it works yet."

"It looks so pretty."

"But if it doesn't work, it's just a huge paperweight."

Aerie shrugged. Like she would almost keep it even if it were just a decorative paperweight. She picked up the electrical cord and plugged it in. Nothing happened. "Let's turn it on."

"Here it is." I flipped the switch on the side of the machine. A set of lights came on inside, like little spotlights to showcase the future popcorn. "That's cool," I admitted. "Do you have any popcorn?"

"I have some at the house. I'll be right back." Aerie left the diner. It was late afternoon, long after we usually close for the day. So, we wouldn't see any customers. But I could easily see everyone would enjoy fresh popcorn. We could offer it while they waited for their orders. I had to hand it to Aerie. This popcorn machine was a good find.

"Got it!" She huffed, out of breath and placed the plastic bag on the counter. "Brand-new."

"That was fast." I looked up. The ready light turned off. "It looks like it has heated up to the right temperature. Let me get some oil." I found coconut oil in the kitchen.

Soon we had fresh popped popcorn and the diner smelled like a movie theater.

"This stuff is great," I said.

Aerie grinned with a mouthful. "I told you."

I nodded. "You did. You were right going to the recycling center paid off. Maybe not for my kitchen, but it's good to be open to the universe for small surprises."

"It's late and while the popcorn is keeping me from starving, I really need a shower." Working for Aerie at the diner had its perks. Smelling like fryer oil wasn't one of them.

"Do you think you'd want to go for pizza?" Aerie asked innocently.

"You want to see Sam, don't you?" Sam, the owner of

The Pizza Pub had been by the diner a few times this week just to chat with Aerie.

She nodded.

"I'm feeling hungry for pizza. Let me shower and I'll pick you up at your place."

ON THE WALK BACK HOME, I noticed the dark gray Ford 150 truck was parked in front of my house. Aerie's brother Jay was still working on the construction of the kitchen. I opened my front door and stepped inside. My little pup Ozzy and the all-knowing Arnold greeted me with yips and kitty-rubs at my ankles.

Taco squawked in the corner to get my attention.

"Hey, Taco, how's it going?"

"Hubba, hubba."

I shook my head. He only 'hubba hubba-ed' when he saw me or Aerie, never for one of the guys. My sexist birdy was a new addition to my crazy family of foster pets. Finding a new home for a scarlet macaw with Taco's skill set was a tough prospect.

Ozzy yipped and panted, excited that I was home. I scratched her behind the ears and rubbed her belly. I stroked Arnold's long black fur but cut the neck rub short.

Hey, I think you just shorted me the extra scratches.

"Extra scratches only happen when I don't get a bill for the vet in Philly."

Ah, my kittens.

"Yes. Exactly." I gave him treats anyway because he was Arnold. The kitten countdown had begun and we were three weeks away from becoming kitten parents.

When can I eat the bird? He's too loud.

5

"You are not allowed to eat Taco." Even though I agreed that the bird was way too loud, I looked closely at Arnold hoping he was just kidding. He wouldn't, would he? I set a small pile of treats on the floor for him. Best keep his kitty belly full.

I sighed. First things first. The kitchen renovation.

Usually, Jay would come by when his job was finished for the day. I was grateful for whatever time he could put in. It wasn't so long ago that he had refused to set foot in my house because we were arguing over whether his girlfriend, Chelsea, had poisoned a Soup and Scoop customer.

Aerie and I thoroughly believed it, mostly because of her past experience being Aerie's middle school bully. But things changed once she helped us find the true killer, and we were all learning to get along, mostly.

Today, the diner had been especially busy. After almost two weeks of a handful of customers, due to the aforementioned murder/poisoning at the diner, it was a welcome relief to be so busy that we didn't even notice the passing of time. All of a sudden it was 2 p.m. and closing time.

I still hadn't added soup back to the menu. Which was saying a lot for a diner named the Soup and Scoop. I had been focusing more on the "Scoop" aspect and new ice cream ideas. Heading to the recycle center had been Aerie's idea of fun. I had to admit it was in a way, but now I was exhausted.

As much as I wanted to get off my feet, I went outside and around to the back of the house to see how the kitchen was coming along.

I pulled out my disheveled ponytail and shook my hair loose to my shoulders. I still had a bit of a crush on Jay, even if I didn't want to admit it.

The kitchen protruded like a fresh framed box. "Hey, there. How's it going?" I shouted over the sound of the nail gun.

Jay stepped out from behind the framed wall, shirtless. My breath caught in my throat. Crush magnified. I let out the air stuck in my throat and sighed. "How's it going?" I attempted not to ogle by putting on a friendly smile.

His grin at me made it worse. I took another deep breath.

"It's great. The kitchen is framed out and ready for drywall. Do you know what kind of cabinets you'll want?"

Nope, not at all, actually, but I told him, "I'm still thinking it over."

The idea of purchasing all the cabinets in one go made my savings account weep silently. And then there were the appliances. I got dizzy just thinking about it.

A wave of concern swept over Jay's features. "You okay?" He quickly put down the nail gun, ready to catch me.

I steadied myself against the side of the house and laughed it off. "Yeah, yeah. Just tired from working at the diner."

His grin returned. "Business is back?"

"And then some. I think Mrs. Orsa brought the entire historical society in for breakfast today."

"Ha. I'll try to bring the guys from the site over for lunch tomorrow."

"Where are you working this week?"

"At Miller's Barn. He needs a new shed. Actually, it's an extra-large chicken coop."

"Really? So, I guess you guys aren't using the crane I saw driving down Main yesterday?"

"That would be for the theater going in at the Spring

7

Creek Plaza. An old friend of mine is the general contractor over there."

"Are they almost done?"

"I think so, they're hanging the signage today."

There was an awkward silence, and we both stood there.

"So, how's the kitchen coming? You mentioned drywall?" I walked over and picked a dandelion out of the lawn. "I had to chase some squirrels out of here the other morning." I pointed to my incomplete kitchen.

He bent down, picked up his t-shirt, and shook it out. "Yep." He pulled the t-shirt over his head. "I just need to get one of my guys to come with me to pick it up and we can have it installed pretty quickly. About half a day or so. Not long."

"Wow, I might actually have walls again."

"Yeah, I can pull out that plywood board between the rest of the house and you won't have to come out here to see your kitchen or worry about squirrels."

"I'd make some joke about how this would force me to cook, but you know..." He knew I cooked all morning at his sister's diner. He owned a stake in the diner too; he just never mentioned it.

"Well, you'll now be able to relax in a sunny kitchen sipping your coffee before you come to the diner."

"That would be nice. I can't thank you enough for helping out with this, Jay."

"No problem, really. It feels good to do something for someone. And I feel bad about Chelsea..."

He didn't have to spell out that he felt bad about Chelsea connecting her right hook to my left cheek a few weeks back. She had barely hit me. "It's all water under the bridge."

"Yeah? I hope so."

"Even Aerie is warming up to her. The other day she offered her a blueberry muffin on the house."

Jay chuckled. "I heard. Chelsea said it confused her. She wasn't sure if Aerie was being nice or if she should accuse her of wanting her to gain weight."

"Sounds about right. Hey, do you want a soda?"

"Nah, I'll finish up here and head out. I'm taking Chelsea out for her birthday."

"Where are you guys going?"

"I wanted to take her somewhere in the city, something nice, so we're going over to Linguini's. It's an Italian restaurant near the capitol building."

"That should be nice. Well, I'll let you get back to work. Thanks again, Jay."

"Yeah, no problem." He disappeared back into the frame of the kitchen where he put the nail gun back to use as I made my way to the front of the house. Jay was pretty much occupied by Chelsea. So even though he was the most generous and sweet, not to mention handsome, guy I knew in town, I would have to let that crush go and focus on friendship.

My stomach rumbled. Heading to the pizza place wasn't such a bad idea. Maybe I wouldn't be having a date at Linguini's anytime soon, but I had a feeling Aerie might, if she played her cards right. And I, as her best friend, was here to help.

I MADE sure to feed everyone, namely Arnold, before I headed out. Ozzy got her bowl of kibble and I didn't want Taco to feel left out so I gave him some fresh seed. The house was beginning to feel like a menagerie of pets. I hopped in the car and headed over to pick up Aerie.

She jumped in looking as zen as usual. Probably all the yoga. But I thought I recognized some lip gloss and a bit of rouge on her cheeks.

"So, I hear Jay is taking Chelsea to Linguini's tonight." I waited for her to click her seatbelt before heading toward the plaza.

"Is that right?" The angst in her voice wasn't lost on me.

"He didn't tell you?" Jay and Aerie were close siblings so I was a bit surprised that he hadn't mentioned it to her.

"No. I think he still believes I'll react badly to news of their relationship."

"Like that hasn't happened in the past," I sarcastically added.

"Well, I'm over it. I've been meditating on this, and I've come to terms with the fact that Jay lo—likes Chelsea. And that they are together. My brother has his own life."

"I think I see your teeth grinding."

"Oh, please. It's hard enough. I still can't stand her. And she can't stand me, so it's even ground."

"Just call me when there's a catfight," I said.

"You know she'd be the one to start it."

"And you would finish it."

"You've got that right," she said with conviction.

I snorted through my nose. I had no doubt that sweet Aerie could hold her own. She rarely got angry but when she did, oh boy.

"So, Sam has been by the diner quite a bit lately," I hinted.

She grinned to herself. "Oh, I hadn't noticed."

"You can't be coy with me. How is it going?"

"He's very nice."

"Nice? That's all I get? Come on, spill it." I couldn't wait to hear her put words to her emotions.

"He is very sweet. And I like him. He has also started carrying vegan cheese for his pizzas."

"A suggestion from his new 'girlfriend'?"

"We're not boyfriend and girlfriend, yet."

I nodded. "'Yet' is the operative term. I bet you guys will be officially together by the end of the week." I could confidently say this because I was determined to see it happen.

"I wouldn't have any objection to that."

"Sweet. The game is on. I'll have him asking you out by next Friday."

She shifted quickly in her car seat to look at me. "No, no. Don't push him into it. I want it to happen naturally."

"You sound like a laxative ad."

"I do not. Just leave him alone. I can make sure we end up on a date by next Friday."

"I see how it is." I smiled. Once Aerie sets her mind to something she always makes it happen.

I pulled into the parking lot expecting to find the crane hovering over the newly built theater addition to the plaza, but there were only a few pickup trucks and cars in the lot.

The sign wasn't up either. It sat crookedly next to the entrance of the theater. Yellow caution tape was tacked to the cones across the sidewalk, prohibiting entry to the work site. The Pizza Pub's entrance was right next to the construction. Sam had been thrilled when he got the approval to open his wall into the theater entrance. Late-night moviegoers equaled lots of pizza orders.

The intoxicating scent from the pizza ovens engulfed us as we walked in.

"Hello, my favorite ladies!" Sam called out.

Aerie practically beamed like sunshine.

"Hey, Sam. I talked Aerie into coming over for dinner. She said you had some new vegan cheese you're trying out."

"Yes, I do. Would you like some on your pizza, Mira?"

"Ah, no. I'm not there yet."

"Got it. So, what will it be?"

Aerie leaned slightly into the counter never taking her eyes off of Sam's. "Can I get a small gluten-free vegan with mushroom?" Aerie smitten? Adorable.

"Absolutely, my dear." Sam looked to me. "And what can I get for you?"

"Can I get a large, regular cheese, with onions and peppers?"

"Will do. I should have these up in twenty minutes, ladies. Please have a seat." He waved an inviting hand around the dining area. "Any one you want."

Aerie and I chose the booth closest to the counter. Aerie, of course, sat on the side where she could stare at Sam, and I faced the entrance, unfortunately giving me a clear view of Detective Lockheart striding into the restaurant.

I pushed myself as tightly as possible into the corner of the booth, whispering, "Don't turn around, Detective Lockheart just came in."

"What?" Aerie twisted in her seat to look. The detective caught the movement and saw us.

"Why am I not surprised?" he said with an exasperated look on his face. He practically rolled his eyes.

"We're allowed to have dinner, aren't we?" I grumbled.

"No. Not when it's at a crime scene."

At those words Sam came back to the counter. "What's this about? A crime scene?"

"Hey, Sam. I'm just here to ask a few questions about the theft that occurred at the work site this morning."

"This is the first I've heard of any theft." He dusted off his hands.

"I got the call early this morning from the general contractor. It seems the crane has been removed from the property."

"The crane? That's impressive," Sam said. I heartily agreed.

"It's not impressive; it's theft. Anyway, I need to ask you a few questions. Did you see anything suspicious last evening?"

Sam stood there a moment, thinking. "Most days, the crew comes in for lunch. But last night, one of the guys came in for dinner."

Dan pulled out his notebook and scribbled with a pencil. "And who would that be?"

"The guy named Travis. He stayed late, had a lot of beers. I called him a cab."

"What time would you say you called the cab?"

"Hmm. Think it was about ten-thirty."

Dan scribbled in his note pad. "Is there anything else you can think of? Anything that was out of the ordinary?"

Sam paused a moment before continuing. "Yeah, I guess I was surprised Travis didn't have his truck parked out front. He was going to need a ride home whether he had been drinking or not."

Dan scribbled additional notes and closed his notebook, shoving the pencil into the wire coil and cramming the entire thing into his back pocket.

"Thanks, Sam. I appreciate your time." He reached out a hand and Sam shook it, forgetting that he had a hand covered in flour. They laughed as the detective shook off the flour and Sam handed him a few napkins.

"Sorry about that."

"Not a problem. Have a good evening Sam." Detective Lockheart turned to go but stopped mid-stride in front of our table. "And you." He pointed a finger at me. Something I hated. "No. That's all I have to say. Just, no." He stalked out before I could come up with any kind of witty retort.

He made me so mad. Aerie patted my arm and smiled. I looked at her. "What are you smiling at? He's such a jerk."

She nodded and smiled. "Yep," she said, without any conviction.

A few moments later, Sam walked over with our pizzas. With great flourish, he set them on our table. He even handed us cloth napkins. I grinned to myself. Cloth napkins instead of paper? Another influence from his soon-to-be girlfriend.

2

The scent of popcorn wafted through the diner. I tightened my apron strings and pulled the stainless-steel cup from the milkshake machine. My mouth watered in anticipation. I grabbed one of the ice cream scoops, opened the freezer chest and leaned over to scoop out the chocolate raspberry swirl. Once the cup was half-full, I took some whole milk from the glass-fronted fridge and filled the cup. I added a good squirt of chocolate syrup, put the cup back into the milkshake machine, and flipped the switch on top. The happy buzz of the blender caught Aerie's attention and she walked away from a table to meet me. "What are you up to?" Aerie usually handled the front of the diner and the drinks.

"I wanted to see how this new ice cream flavor tasted as a shake."

"And?"

"Let's see." I removed the stainless-steel cup and picked up a shake straw and poured the mixture into a tall glass. The frothy thick chocolate filled the glass faster than I expected and it almost ended on the floor. I jammed in the straw and slurped, swallowing quickly. "It tastes really good." I brought my other hand up to my forehead and pressed hard with the palm of my hand. "Brain freeze."

"Serves you right for not pouring it into two glasses."

"This one's not vegan, you know."

"It looks yummy. I want to know what it tastes like."

"My next recipe will be with oat milk." The headache faded and I pulled my hand away from my face.

Aerie took a small sip. "Oh, I forgot how heavy milk is, but it's very tasty. Good job on the raspberry. I'll mention it to the customers as today's special." She pointed to the chalkboard, listing the burger orders she just took for the lunch crowd.

The bell rang at the diner entrance and we both looked over. Sam Andrews walked in. Aerie lit up like the sun.

"You can handle this. I'll be in the kitchen."

She didn't say anything, only nodded. All her attention focused on Sam. It was so darn cute I couldn't help but smile. Besides, there were some hamburgers that needed to be flipped.

The lunch crowd kept me busy cooking fries and hamburgers. I said a quick note of gratitude to the universe for sending us our customers, especially after the supposed poisoning, which luckily had been cleared up. I tried to listen in on Aerie's conversation with Sam, but I was too far away to hear actual words. The concern in his voice was easy to interpret—after all, I lived in a construction zone; he worked next to one. When the burgers were prepped and ready to head out to the front, I walked them out myself.

"While I'm getting business from the contractors, the construction keeps out my regulars. The sooner the construction tape and equipment is gone, the sooner I can get customers coming back in."

Aerie nodded knowingly. The police activity around the diner after the poisoning caused a huge dip in our customer numbers. There were days when only dear Mrs. Orsa came in.

The bell over the door rang again, this time to announce Detective Lockheart. I looked up to heaven and mouthed, 'Why?' I headed back into the kitchen as Aerie took his order. Hamburger, fries, and a shake. Every time.

I slapped another burger on the grill and dropped a basket of fries. The shake machine whirred out front. I wasn't coming out of the kitchen until Detective Lockheart finished his lunch and left the building.

I heard him ask about the popcorn maker. However, he used an accusatory tone. I walked out to stand with Aerie.

"Isn't it great? We picked it up at the recycle center yesterday," she said.

"Yesterday? At the recycle center?" Dan pulled out his notebook.

"That's what she said. We found it at the recycle center and we brought it back here and cleaned it up," I told him.

"You cleaned it?" For some reason Dan's tone made it sound like we were ignorant fools.

"Of course we cleaned it. I wasn't going to have something that had spent time on the asphalt of the recycle center on the counter here at the diner without a good bleaching."

"You bleached it?"

"Detective Lockhart. What part of 'we cleaned it' do you not understand?"

Dan closed his eyes and took a deep breath. "Noah Weller, the owner of the theater, reported a popcorn machine being stolen from the property yesterday." He looked at Aerie and then at me. "The two of you don't know anything about that?"

"Of course we don't." I put my hands on my hips. "Are you insinuating we stole the popcorn maker?" I practically screeched and a few customers looked concerned as they glanced at us.

Dan took another controlled breath. "No." He wrote in his notebook.

Aerie leaned across the counter toward him. "Dan, you know me. I wouldn't steal a popcorn maker. I wouldn't steal anything. We got this at the recycle center and we can take you there and show you where we found it. Won't we, Mira?"

"Not until we're done with the lunch rush and have cleaned and closed up the diner." My hands were still on my hips, and I'm pretty sure I did a hair toss, even with the hairnet over my ponytail.

"I'll wait." Dan settled into his stool at the counter, obviously prepared to wait as long as he needed to. That's when I smelled something burning in the kitchen and rushed back to the grill.

Dan's hamburger and fries were a little overcooked, okay burnt. It was the one time in the history of me cooking at the diner that I served food that was less than my best. I only felt slightly guilty when he winced but ate the burger anyway.

AFTER WE RETURNED the popcorn machine to Mr. Weller at the theater, Dan offered to take us to the recycle center in his patrol car. I flatly refused and drove Aerie and myself. We parked in the lot and Dan asked us to show him step-by-step everything we did yesterday.

"I don't remember everything," I told him.

"We can give Dan a rough estimate of what we did." Aerie gave me a slight scowl and then spoke to Dan. "We walked through the parking lot and we went right to the Freecycle area to look for something for Mira's kitchen."

Dan raised an eyebrow and looked at me. I shrugged. "I walked over here—" I noticed a few items that weren't there yesterday, but nothing stood out— "And that's when I noticed the red paint shining in the sun—" I walked around the closest pile, "and found the popcorn machine under a bag of clothes."

Dan pointed to a nearby trash bag. "Was it this bag?"

"I have no idea." For some reason, I always felt like I was failing some exam with him.

Detective Lockheart called over Officer Stewart to gather evidence. He directed the officer to the plastic bag. The detective continued to scan the area, obviously looking for something. "And you didn't see anything suspicious?" He looked up from his notes.

"Other than a brand-new shiny popcorn maker sitting at the Freecycle center?" I sweetly asked.

He glared at me.

"No, we didn't see anything."

"No Dan, once we found the popcorn machine, we brought it to the diner," Aerie told him.

"How did you get it there?"

"What kind of question is that? We put it in the back of my Buick," I told him matter-of-factly.

"I found some bungee cords to tie down the trunk," Aerie added.

Dan took a deep breath and let it out in a huff. "Can I see the trunk of your car?"

While officer Stewart was busy collecting the disgusting evidence of old clothes in ratty trash bags, Detective Dan leaned over the inside of my trunk using his pen to prod and poke it things.

"What exactly are you doing?" I asked.

"Nothing that should concern you."

"What is that supposed to mean? You know we didn't steal the popcorn machine."

He stood up, squared off his feet, and looked me in the eye. "The fact that the two of you are, yet again, involved in criminal activity in this town, is utterly unbelievable that it could be a coincidence. At the same time, I know Aerie, and by default, you..." I glared at him. "I know neither of you would have stolen the popcorn machine, however it is my job as Detective to take every single step I can to find out who did."

He walked away and began to take notes, occasionally looking up and searching the area.

Aerie stood next to me. "He's just doing his job."

"He doesn't have to be a jerk about it."

"Dan is just super-serious." Aerie nudged my shoulder.

"Why are you nudging me?"

"Because I think if you give Dan a break, you might see some nice things about him."

"I see where you're going. Put a stop to it right now. You are the one dating, not me." I enunciated the "not me" very slowly so she would understand what I was getting at. There was no way I was dating Dan Lockheart.

"Ladies, can I have your attention for a moment over here?" Dan called from a muddy patch of grass at the edge of the recycle center lot.

Aerie headed toward the area. I reluctantly pushed myself off the Buick where I had been resting. Dan stood over the muddy patch that held a large impression of a tire tread. "Did either of you see this when you were here?"

"No."

"Nope."

Detective Lockhart thought for a moment then scanned the area where the piles were located. "Walk with me," he said.

Aerie followed. I let out a big sigh and followed.

"Do either of you notice any new additions to the lot since yesterday?" he asked.

"No," Aerie said.

I cleared my throat. "There were a few small items I noticed that were new from yesterday."

"But nothing large?" He pointed to some of the bigger appliances that sat under the awning. "Those items were here yesterday?"

"Yes. All of this was here before. Like I said, only small stuff. I can point them out to you." I gestured to them. "That wooden salad bowl and that box of books. That's all I notice now that is new since we were here yesterday."

Dan nodded and took notes furiously in his notebook. "Very good." When he was done scribbling, he looked up. "This might be a track from the crane, or a vehicle that picked up the crane. This is great evidence. Thank you very much, ladies. You can both go."

I shook my head. I hated being dismissed like that. But I was glad to be leaving. Secretly I was a little smug that we had helped to find new evidence.

ONCE WE GOT in the car, Aerie sighed. "Sam is stressing about the delay in the theater's opening."

"Really?"

"Yes. Since construction began, his revenue has been down. And now that it's halted, who knows how long it will take?"

"Does he have any idea who stole the equipment?"

"No. But they're having a problem getting a new crane to the site. The owner doesn't want to open the theater without it."

"You want to go looking for the crane?" I sat up straighter as I drove. "How hard can it be to find a crane? I mean, how do you lose something that huge in the first place?"

"If we found it, it would help Sam." Aerie perked up. "It's kind of like our other mysteries, only without the death."

"Exactly! Let's find this thing."

"You're pretty gung-ho about finding a piece of construction equipment."

"It's the one thing I know Detective Lockheart doesn't want me to do. Besides you saw how some of the customers looked at us when Dan blurted out the popcorn machine was stolen. It wouldn't hurt if we find the crane to remind everyone what side of the law we're on." I rubbed my hands together.

"So, of course, you want to do it."

"Of course. And I know the only reason you want to find this thing is to make Sam happy." I nudged her in the ribs.

"Oh, be quiet. But yes."

We decided to look for clues at the last place the crane was seen: the theater parking lot.

That's when, out of the blue, Aerie brought up my least

favorite person. "It's awfully nice of Dan to come by and have lunch at the diner every day."

"What are you talking about? He's keeping tabs on me to make sure I'm not investigating any crimes."

"Is he?"

I gave her a look. But she was busy looking out the window. "What else is he doing?"

"Oh, I don't know. I just think it's nice of him to come by. He was supportive of us during the poison investigation."

"He was not. He arrested me. As if you don't remember."

"He was keeping you safe."

"Hardly. He was getting his own way. Trying to 'teach me a lesson' for making him 'look bad'." I raised my fingers in air quotes.

"Well, I'm mostly talking about him supporting the diner."

"Good for him. I'm glad he spent his money at your diner."

"Our diner."

"I'm just a cook, Jay owns the diner with you."

"Well, about that..."

I turned and looked at her again incredulous but then realizing I should have expected it. Jay had been wanting to get out of the diner business for a while to focus on his construction business.

"I was wondering if you wanted to go in on the diner with me when Jay leaves."

"What? I mean, thanks. You barely know me. How can you offer me half of your own diner?"

"I just know you're the right person." She kept her eyes on the road.

I tried to soften the blow. "I love it here. Don't get me

wrong. But I always figured I would flip the Victorian and with that money purchase another house somewhere else."

Even focused on the road in front of us, I could see she was thinking about it.

"Maybe ask me again in another month?"

Aerie smiled and just nodded. "Okay." I could tell she wouldn't forget. She was probably putting it on her mental calendar.

I changed the subject fast. "So, what did Sam say about the crane and the workers? Anything suspicious?"

Aerie took a deep breath. "We should talk to the construction workers. He said some of his interactions with them have felt a little off."

"What does he mean by 'off'?"

"Just weird, I guess. He thinks that something is going on. I asked Jay about it. He knows the general contractor, Karl Simpson. I think he used to work with him when they were younger."

"Anything we should know?"

"Jay says he's a nice guy. But he just went through a really nasty divorce and he had a hard time finding work after that. And Jay was surprised to find out that Karl got this big, commercial job."

"Okay, that's interesting. I guess we could start there. I'm not sure how easy it will be to interview the men while they're working."

"I was thinking, if you don't mind, we could wait and eat at Sam's and see if any of the men come in. He says they might come in for dinner or at least a beer before they head home."

I smiled. Aerie deserved all the happiness in the world. "Pizza for dinner sounds perfect." Hopefully there was lots of pizza in Aerie's future.

As we turned into the parking lot, the heavy clouds that had threatened since this morning opened up. It was one of those early summer showers that were torrential but most of the time short-lived. I parked. It was three-thirty. We had half an hour before the construction crew would call it a day. I could see that most of the work was being done inside the theater. So, the rain didn't affect them.

"You want to sit for a bit?"

"Yeah, let's see if it calms down. If we get out now, we'll get soaked."

Sitting in the car together after I turned her down was a little more than awkward. I tried to fill the space with chatter. "We know Sam. But do you know the other owners of the other businesses here?"

Aerie pointed to the left. "The hardware store is owned by Bob Earl. He's owned it since I was little. Nice guy. The day spa, have you been in there? It's a great place to get your hair cut. I think it's owned by someone with the last name Greer. The paint-your-own-pottery is owned by an old friend of mine named Heather Gerry, then Sam's place, and the theater."

"After talking with the workers, we should also talk to the other business owners and see if they heard or saw anything the night of the theft."

Aerie rubbed her hands together. "We're becoming regular private investigators."

"Don't let Detective Lockheart hear you. "

I pulled my hair out of the ponytail. "I was thinking of getting my hair cut soon anyway. We have time to kill. Think they take walk-ins?"

"They do. Should we see if they have availability? I don't need a cut, but when I do, Cara Summers is the one I see. She'd do a great job on your hair, too."

"Worth a shot." I grinned. I guess I was getting my hair cut sooner than I thought. "Want to come with me?"

"Well, I don't want to sit in this car all afternoon."

"Ready to brave the rain?"

"Let's do it."

3

We exited the car quickly. The humid heat from the parking lot rose up around my legs while the cool fat raindrops pelted my head. We ran across the lot to the overhang in front of the day spa. I pulled open the door and chivalrously waved Aerie in first. The cool air-conditioned air chilled my rain-soaked skin.

One of the women in the spa came out from the back carrying two towels. "Here you go ladies, dry yourselves off. It's cats and dogs out there."

"More like drowned rats." Chelsea sat at the salon table getting her nails done by a disinterested nail technician.

Aerie flinched but ignored the barb and greeted the woman. "Hi Cara. I brought my friend Mira; she's hoping for a cut."

Cara looked at me and shook my hand. "Welcome. Good timing! I can fit you in right now."

I toweled off my arms and face. "Thanks Cara, I really appreciate it."

"Hey Mira," Chelsea called out. "Were you able to wash the scent of jail cell off after your recent visit?"

"Jay says hi, he was at my house earlier," I fibbed just to see if she would squirm.

"Oh, I'm not worried about Jay. As you can see, I'm getting my nails done so when he pops the question, the closeup selfie will be fabulous."

Aerie made a retching sound. I grabbed her arm and pulled her closer to the hairdressing sinks.

Cara wanted to clear the air as well. "Right this way." She ushered us toward the chairs. "Your last cut is holding up well, Aerie. How are things?"

"Good. Just working at the diner. Business has been up, which keeps us busy."

"Right. That poisoning last month was crazy. It's good to hear that you're doing better." I heard a faint retort at the front of the salon and hoped that Chelsea's nails would dry faster.

"Yeah, everything is back to normal. How are things here?" Aerie leaned against the sinks.

"Going pretty well. But I have to tell you I think we'll all be happier when that theater finishes construction." Cara waved me toward a cushioned seat near the sinks. "We'll wash your hair first. I have some new conditioner that's amazing."

"Sam told me there was some issue with construction and that it's taking more time than they thought it would." Aerie was getting better at this investigating thing.

"Yeah, like someone stole the crane. Who does that kind of stuff?" Cara grabbed a towel and turned on the water behind me.

"You got me," I added.

"What kind of cut are you looking for today, Mira?"

"Just a trim. Maybe about two inches?"

"Let's get you washed up and we'll take a look." Cara draped a cape around me. "Like, really, how can they lose a giant crane?"

"Sam's upset about it. He says the construction is keeping people away."

"For sure. Business is definitely slow here too. The sooner the construction is done the better off we'll be. But if they can't finish without the crane..."

"I think they're looking for new equipment at this point," Aerie added.

"Crazy, I tell you. How's your summer going so far, Mira?" Cara massaged conditioner into my hair and rinsed.

"Good. Jay says he'll be able to have the walls up in my kitchen by the end of the week, with a new door and everything."

"That's right, you own the old Spencer house. You're brave."

"It's not so bad. Jay's been helping a lot."

"I heard about the fire. And Becca's murder. Killed in your kitchen. You're not afraid of sleeping in that house?" She towel-dried my hair and directed me to a chair near the mirrors.

"Nah, I just tell the ghosts to mind their own business." Little did she know how true that was.

"Braver than me, that's for sure. Okay, let's comb this out." She gently combed my curls and took out her scissors.

Aerie followed us. "So, Cara, how have you been?"

"I'm doing well. My son turns seven next week."

"Oh congratulations. Are you doing anything special?"

"I'm thinking of having his party at the pottery place next door. He loves making a mess with paint lately."

"Now you're the brave one." Aerie laughed.

"That may be." Cara finished combing my hair. "So, Mira, do you part your hair on the right or the left?"

"Actually, the center. If you could make my bangs a little shorter that would be great."

"Will do." Cara pulled some of my wet hair back in clips and began to cut.

"I suppose you have a lot of clients that come in and just talk about their lives," I started.

"Sure," she continued combing and cutting.

"Have you noticed lately if anyone's upset about the construction of the theater?"

Before Cara could answer, a woman came out from the back of the salon dressed in a pantsuit that was obviously designer. Her hair and makeup were done impeccably. "Cara, we make it a point not to share our client's information."

"Oh, I'm sorry. I didn't mean to pry," I said. The woman grinned, accepting my apology.

"Where is the reservation book for this week?" she asked Cara.

"It's on the reception desk right there. We have a few more reservations for the couples massage in the evening."

The woman nodded, walked over to the front desk, marked the book, closed it, and tucked it under her arm, and walked back into the offices at the rear of the salon.

"Is that the owner?" I asked.

"Yeah, that's Ilsa. I don't know why she said that, she gossips more than I do." Cara clipped away with the scissors.

"I love her pantsuit. I could never pull that off."

"I couldn't either. You have to be pretty tall and long-waisted." After a few more moments of freeing my hair from the clips and cutting, Cara was finished. "There we go. What do you think about the length of your bangs?"

"Looks good." I admired my haircut in the mirror.

"A quick blow dry?"

"Sure. Although I don't know how that'll fair in this weather." Humidity always did a number on my curls.

Aerie chimed in, "You have a hairdryer at home, don't you?"

"Ha, ha." I fake laughed.

Once Cara was finished with my hair, I paid her with a cash tip. Thankfully Chelsea was nowhere to be found.

The rain had slowed to a sprinkle and we made it back to the car without getting too wet. "Cara couldn't give us any information about her clients."

"You were expecting somebody more like Ellie?" Aerie mentioned our friend, the bank teller, who shared everybody's information with everybody else.

"Yeah, I was hoping. Too bad. At least I got a good haircut. Do you like it?"

"You look fabulous."

WE ENTERED THE PIZZA PUB. Aerie followed behind me. "Hey Sam, how's it going?"

"Good evening ladies. Can I get the two of you something?"

"You know I'll always eat your pizza. I'll have a small Hawaiian," I said.

"And for you, the beautiful Aerie?"

I snorted. Aerie actually blushed. "Can I get the gluten-free, vegan, mushroom personal pizza?"

"Anything for you." He winked.

"You guys are too cute for words," I said sarcastically, and headed to a booth to let the lovebirds chat privately. I looked at the list I had started on my phone. The suspect list. Crazy that we had developed a private-eye routine. Question possible witnesses; create a suspect list. Aerie and I were getting good at this. There's nothing like a concise suspect list.

Right now, the list consisted of everyone who owned businesses in the plaza. Tonight I would add each of the workers' names to the list. And probably include some description next to it, also known as "reasons why" or "motive".

Movement across the room distracted me from my phone. A lanky teen was setting up some audio equipment.

"Hey, Sam?" I shouted to them from the booth. "Are you having a band tonight?"

"Not tonight. Tonight is karaoke."

Aerie turned to me with a sly grin. Her grey eyes twinkled.

"Oh, no you don't. I am not singing," I warned her.

"Come on, it'll be fun," she pleaded, cheerfully.

"People's ears will bleed if I sing." I have never been able to carry a tune.

"That's part of the fun."

I don't think she quite understood how seriously tone deaf I was. "What if everybody ends up in the ER?"

"Ha ha, very funny."

I gave in. "Sam, I think you'll need to add a beer to my order."

"That, I can do." He leaned across the counter. "Hey, Scott!" He dusted off his hands and walked around to the dining room. "Let me introduce you to Scott."

Scott came out from the small side room that opened into the dining room. He was tall and skinny, and he looked like he was probably about twenty.

"Hey." He smiled from ear to ear and reached out his hand to shake ours. "I'm Scott. I'm here for the summer."

"Home from school?"

"Yep, I go to Penn State, I'm a food science major."

Sam chuckled. "He's here to learn how to make pizza from the best." He squeezed Scott's shoulder. "Aren't you, kid?"

Scott smiled. "You need all the help you can get, old man."

"Watch who you're calling an old man." He laughed again. "Did you get all of the karaoke speakers set up?"

"Almost all of it. It should be a fun night."

"Especially if we can get Mira to do this thing," Sam joked.

"Like I said, only if you want people visiting the ER." I was serious about not singing.

By the time we got our pizzas, the workers were filing in from next door. Travis, who was a little heavyset, and this skinny guy I didn't know yet were the first to arrive. Behind them was the general contractor, Karl, whom Jay knew. With him was another guy, medium build, dark blond. The last guy, thinner medium build with dark hair, came in by himself and it looked to me like he preferred it that way.

I took out my phone and listed the workers #1, #2, #3, #4 and Karl. At some point during the evening, Aerie and I would have to talk to each of them.

She and I finished our meal, and I nursed my beer while she sipped her iced tea. We covertly watched the guys. Unfortunately, nobody had a neon sign above their head flashing: I stole the crane!

They sucked down beers during their meals, while I sipped mine. Hopefully that would loosen their lips, and we could get some good information. After another hour, the place was full of customers. This obviously was the place to come on a Friday evening.

Sam and Scott were busy in the back kitchen frying chicken wings and pulling pizzas out of the oven. At some point the room became more of a standing room than a dining room and Aerie grabbed my wrist and dragged me into the alcove with the karaoke equipment.

There was a small stage in the corner with karaoke speakers on either side, and a mic stand in the middle. All of this created a sinking feeling of dread.

"I'm not getting up there," I told her.

"We'll see."

"You go first." Because I thought she wouldn't dare to do it.

"Okay." She marched right to the stage stepped up and grabbed the mic. She pushed some buttons on the karaoke machine and the speakers turned on. I guessed she had done this before. Feedback from the mic got everybody's attention and the room quieted down. She turned on the music and as it played the song, *Love is All We Need*, she stepped back to the mic stand and closed her eyes, swaying to the beat.

Aerie opened her mouth, and graceful melodic song graced our ears. Slowly the room quieted even more, everyone stopped just to listen to her. My feelings of dread turned to pride watching my friend captivate an entire room. Talk about brave! I leaned back to see Sam's response to the song choice—clearly it was directed at him—but from this angle I couldn't see him. I imagined he was getting the point. If he didn't, I would make sure to bring it up later.

As Aerie finished, the room exploded in applause. She bowed with a curtsy and stepped off the stage.

And handed me the mic.

"Are you crazy? Not after that performance." I shook my head. "You were incredible."

"Thank you." She humbly accepted the compliment. "You said you'd go if I did. Go on up."

4

I looked at the mic. "Let me have another beer first."

"Okay, rely on your artificial courage."

"Absolutely. Where's Sam?" I propped the mic back in the stand and we squeezed our way through the crowd to the counter.

Sam handed me another beer with a smile, but his eyes were all on Aerie. "That was a very sweet song you sang."

"Thank you." She actually fluttered her eyelashes.

"I think it was for you," I added. And they stared at me. After an awkward moment of silence, they grinned.

Ah, love. I turned my attention to the suspects at hand and walked over to Travis and the skinny guy to introduce myself. "Hey there. I'm Mira. I work at the diner."

"Yeah, I've seen you. I'm Travis. This is Milo." He took a big swig of his beer. Travis looked like he had been all muscle at some point early in his life, but now he was simply a big guy who had gone soft in the middle. He obviously enjoyed his beer.

Milo nodded and sipped his beer. He shifted nervously from foot to foot.

I decided to simply come out with it. Why mince words? "You guys have any idea who stole the equipment?"

"Who's asking?" Travis took another swig of beer.

"I dunno. I'm just curious. Like, who would steal a giant crane, for crying out loud?"

"I don't know. Maybe some teenagers thinking it's a good prank." Travis laughed and grabbed Milo's shoulder. Milo flinched.

"I want nothing to do with it." He pulled away from Travis. "I need this job and I don't want to get fired because I'm associating with anyone who had something to do with that malarkey."

Travis's happy go lucky demeanor disappeared. "Are you saying I had something to do with it?"

"That's what Ron said." Milo took another small sip of his beer.

Travis looked across the room and glared at the dark-haired loner in the corner. I guessed that was Ron. I made a mental note to add their names to the suspect list along with this juicy bit of information.

Aerie grabbed my wrist and pulled me back toward the karaoke corner.

"Oh no you don't. I'm busy investigating." I hissed in her ear.

"You need to have more fun." She beamed like sunshine. Obviously, Sam was good for her.

"I do not. You're the one that wants to solve the mystery of the missing equipment."

"I do, but we don't need to do it right now. It's your turn to sing."

She pulled the beer out of my hands and replaced it with the mic. She prodded me toward the karaoke corner.

"Go ahead. You can do it." When I refused to step up

onto the stage, she pushed me up and followed me. She programmed something into the karaoke machine. "You know the song, right?"

I glanced over her shoulder and shrugged. "Yeah, I guess."

"Great." She patted me on the back. "Just give it a try." Then she abandoned me.

I looked out at the crowd. Most of them were in private conversations, but a few of them were staring expectantly at me.

Weren't they going to be surprised? I thought.

The music started. I began to sing, so badly. Some of those upturned faces quickly turned back to private conversations. All I wanted was to finish the song so I could jump off the stage...until I realized I had a great view of the entire room. I took a deep breath and belted out the off-key tune, keeping my eyes surveying the crowd. I noticed a disturbance.

Travis approached Ron at a fast clip, his beer belly leading the way. He barreled into Ron with such force that they tripped up onto the stage. Before I could duck out of the way, we went down in a heap. The force knocked the wind out of me. The mic hit the floor. I was pinned into a corner with two fighting guys on top of me—not exactly how I thought this song would end. I had been expecting rotten tomatoes being thrown.

I shoved and shoved, trying to get out of the way. I tried to kick them off of me, but I was still trapped with an all too up-close-and-personal view of their rage.

Travis was determined to get a swing in, and as Ron leaned down, Travis's arm shot out and landed one on Ron's chin. Not hard enough to knock him back, but just enough to light a fire in his eyes. Ron grabbed Travis's shirt-front and yanked him up off of me. And then punched him hard in the jaw. Travis fell sideways half on the stage and half off, his cheek resting on the floor. Karl hollered from the center of the room and made big strides in our direction. The crowd parted like the Red Sea.

Karl was a big guy but not as big as Ron. Still, he held his own, shouting something to Ron that made him stop and storm off, shoving people out of his way. Travis was out cold on the floor. Karl leaned down to put an arm under Travis's shoulder. "Glenn, help me out here, let's get him into a chair."

Travis came around slightly. He blinked several times as if trying to bring the room into focus. He was obviously very drunk—the blinking eyes were bloodshot and red-rimmed. I tried to get up from the corner but struggled. My ribs hurt and my backbone felt like it was bruised. Aerie arrived at my side. She took my arm and waited while I worked through some of the pain. She propped me against the wall then disappeared. In moments, she returned with a glass of water, which I drank down.

The police arrived. An officer stepped into the room. Everything grew silent, as though the air was sucked from the place. Thank goodness this was officer Stewart, and not —ugh, Detective Lockheart. The detective spotted me instantly. "What are you doing here?" were his first words.

I straightened up taller, suddenly regretted it. "Having a life," I choked out. My ribs hurt when I spoke. I winced and rubbed them.

"Are you hurt?" He turned away. "We need some medical assistance here," Detective Lockheart called to the EMTs. He sat down next to me, letting the other officer take statements from the room.

The EMTs appeared and Detective Lockheart waved

them over. They asked me questions and shined a light in my eyes. After determining that I did not have a head trauma or broken ribs, they offered to take me to the ER to get looked at.

"No thanks, if my ribs are only bruised, there's nothing to be done, right?" Detective Lockheart tsked but said nothing else.

They nodded and moved on to Travis. He definitely was worse off. They decided to take him to the ER for evaluation on a possible concussion.

I got Aerie's attention. "See..." I pointed. "I told you they'd be taking someone to the ER."

I WOULD HAVE WELCOMED a hangover instead of the bruised ribs as a reminder of last night. I leaned over the ice cream freezer to place my most recent batch of chocolate raspberry —this one was oat milk based—and my ribs screamed at me. I screamed back, at least in my head.

"Are you okay?" Aerie asked, after I moaned and stood up.

I leaned to my right and tried to stretch the left area of my ribs but that felt even worse. "Yeah," I choked out.

Aerie came up to me and looked me straight in the eye and grabbed both my shoulders. "I will never, I promise, ever, ask you to sing again." Her serious face melted into giggles.

"Ha, ha, very funny. I told you bad things would happen."

"Ah, you sound very precognitive, like your sister."

"I'm not psychic." Although hearing my cat's voice in my

head and occasionally seeing a ghost was psychic-adjacent, and I didn't even want to be in the psychic ballpark.

"Worth a try, it sure would help with the investigation."

"We'll find the crane without the help from the supernatural."

The mention of my sister got me to thinking. She hadn't texted me. She usually knew when crazy stuff was about to go down in my life, and she always tried to micromanage it for me. The last time we talked I had asked her, this time politely, to let me live my life. But I hadn't really expected her to.

I pulled out my phone and checked. No texts from last night or this morning. Instead of feeling liberated, I felt off-kilter. I shoved my phone back into my pocket and tried to forget about it.

Mrs. Orsa came in for her usual breakfast muffin and tea. "The ladies and gentlemen at the historical society agreed that we had the most wonderful brunch here the other day. They wanted me to thank you both."

"Oh, Mrs. Orsa, that's wonderful to hear." Aerie wiped the counters around Mrs. Orsa. I knew she had been nervous about having the group so soon after the poisoning.

"I'm glad that the diner is back to regular business. I told you girls to be patient and see, everything is fine."

"You were right, Mrs. Orsa." Aerie gave me *the eye* across the diner. When business was bad during the poisoning Mrs. Orsa came in each morning and reminded us that it was temporary and that we would eventually get our customers back. And she was right.

I've been favoring my side with the bruised ribs all morning. By lunchtime, I needed to take some anti-inflammatories. They didn't help much.

"You know we could switch gears today? I could do the cooking and you can take orders," Aerie told me.

"But you love socializing and I hate it."

"True. But at least you wouldn't have to pick up any of the heavy food boxes or open the refrigerator door. Don't think I didn't hear you when you moaned that time."

"Sorry. It really hurt." For some reason pulling down on the walk-in refrigerator door lit up my entire left side.

The diner was filling for lunch when the bell rang above the door. I glanced over and saw the person responsible for these bruised ribs. Travis what's-his-name. I wasn't exactly mad at him. Intellectually, I knew it wasn't his fault that Ron guy pushed him into me, but I still felt a totally unexpected level of stress just seeing him in the diner. I was glad I didn't have to make conversation with him. I refused to take Aerie up on her offer.

The diner was busy for lunch and I flipped burgers and made sandwiches trying not to think too much about the bruised ribs. They were like a constant painful hum in the background. Travis lingered at the counter and ordered a milkshake. I came out from the back of the kitchen to see which flavor he chose, and it happened to be the chocolate raspberry. Curious about why he was taking his time with lunch, I hung around.

Travis cleared his throat. "Ms. Michaels." He caught my attention. "Ms. Michaels, I just wanted to apologize for last night. I'm real sorry about falling on you like that."

I was surprised to get an apology. Actually, I was surprised he remembered. He had been pretty drunk. "Thanks. I appreciate the apology. You have to let me know if you like the chocolate raspberry."

He grinned sadly. "Sure. I can't eat at Sam's. That jerk Ron is there, not to mention the new owner of the theater.

He keeps coming by to check on the progress. He hovers like a drone over everybody. It makes me nervous."

I nodded to Aerie, a nod that said, I got this, and revved up the blender. Travis winced at the sound and I smiled sympathetically. Maybe I wouldn't want a hangover like that instead of my bruised ribs. Probably a toss-up. Especially if I'd have to do construction like Travis. Loud noises and someone looking over my shoulder? No thanks.

I walked the milkshake to the counter and sat on the stool next to Travis. The owner of the theater was on my suspect list. Maybe I could get some inside information.

"What's the owner's name?"

"Noah Weller. He's a little weasley kinda guy. Real nervous type."

"Oh yeah? How so?"

"Oh, he's always wringing his hands. Nervous about the money. Which makes me nervous because I think he wants to fire all of us and get a new crew. Especially after what happened with the crane. It doesn't help that Ron keeps telling everybody it was my fault. Of course, the drunk did it."

"Did what?"

"Leave the key for the vandals to steal. Somehow the key for the crane didn't make it into the lock box for the night." He shook his head and ate a big spoonful of the ice cream. "This stuff is really good. You make it?"

"I did. Thanks." I cleaned the counter while Travis finished his ice cream.

"I gotta head back to work. Thanks again and sorry about last night." As Travis exited the diner, Detective Lockheart entered. He pierced Travis with a hard look.

"I hope he apologized to you for last night." Detective Lockheart's eyes followed him until he left the building.

"It wasn't his fault, but if you must know, he came here today specifically to apologize." I wiped the already clean counter.

"He's definitely a suspect," the detective mumbled under his breath.

"He didn't steal the crane," I informed him.

"You can't know that."

"He told me, but more than that, he told me what happened with the keys. They never made it back to the lockbox at the end of the day."

Detective Lockheart pulled out his notepad and scribbled something and stuffed it back in his pocket. "Can I get a hamburger and fries?"

I clenched my fist as I walked back into the kitchen. I was going to have to be very careful not to burn his burger to a crisp.

5

Aerie and I closed the diner at three. After we had cleaned up, Aerie decided to go visit Sam while he was working. I needed to head back home because today was the day Jay was hanging the drywall for my kitchen.

When I arrived home, I found him and his coworker Devon unloading drywall from the truck and heading toward the backyard.

Jay saw me as he was carrying a heavy box of drywall and almost fumbled it. "Wonderful! Great, you're here."

"It's nice to be welcomed home. Usually the cat, dog, and parrot, do a good job but this was spectacular."

"Ha. I get it. Do you have a minute to help me? Devon here has to get back to the job site."

I nodded and followed them behind the house. "Whatever you need. I so appreciate your help."

"Do you think you can help me hold drywall steady?"

"Sure. I have no clue what you just said, but sure."

"It's not hard. I just need you to keep the sheets level while I attach them. You don't have to touch any of the adhesive or the hammer and nails. I promise."

"I'd love to help in any way that I can."

Jay was doing most of this work for free for me. If he needed a hand, I could definitely give it a try.

"Great. Let Devon and me finish unloading the truck then we can get to work."

"Sounds good. I'll just go ahead in and take Ozzy for a quick walk."

Ozzy was so excited to see me that she jumped up and down. Then peed all over the floor. Arnold, who was rubbing his chin on my shin, turned away in disgust and disappeared toward the back of the house. I grabbed Ozzy, tucking her under my arm so she wouldn't walk through the pee and track it all over the floor. With one hand, I cleaned up the mess, set Ozzy back down, then headed to the powder room. Washing my hands, I glanced up at my face in the mirror. The face staring back at me wasn't mine. Her dark hair was pulled back from her face into a sleek bun at her neck. She appeared to be silently amused at my situation.

"Clara?" I whispered as the blood drained and I felt light headed.

She disappeared in a blink. She was gone.

"Did you guys see her?" Arnold and Ozzy sat and stared at me, and only Taco had the nerve to answer. "Sexy lady. Sexyyyyyyyy lady."

Arnold licked his paw. I was convinced he saw her too and was just messing with me.

I grabbed Ozzy's leash with shaky hands, and I stumbled outside, dog in tow. I needed some air.

I'm okay with ghosts. I'm okay with ghosts. The mantra didn't seem to help. She's a friendly ghost. She's a friendly ghost. After all, she'd helped me escape when my house was on fire. I regained some of my composure.

Both Jay and Devon smiled on their way to the street for more drywall. Ozzy desperately wanted to play with them, but I held her back so she wouldn't get tangled in their legs while they were working. "I'll be back in a few."

Poor Ozzy. I dragged her around the block super-fast. At this point, she really didn't have to pee. She had pretty much let it all out on the dining room floor. I didn't want to think about Clara the friendly ghost in my house. The move here was supposed to separate me from my sister's other-worldly *friends*. I was anxious to get back to the kitchen and to help Jay. It meant I could stop staring at the plywood that was nailed over the kitchen entrance in the dining room. I knew it would be a while before I was able to purchase all of the appliances even after the drywall was hung. But at least I would have the room back.

Once back at the house I watched as Devon drove off in Jay's truck.

"You're letting him use your truck?" I knew Jay loved that thing.

"He'll be careful with my baby. He's a good guy."

"I can give you a ride back to...wherever." I realized I didn't know where Jay lived at the moment, since he moved out of the family house he normally shared with Aerie. I supposed he was living with Chelsea, but I wasn't sure where that was.

"No worries, I've been wanting to check in on Aerie."

"Why is that? Is your brotherly protectiveness coming out because she might be seeing someone?"

He grinned. "Maybe." He motioned me to the backyard. I put Ozzy into the house and then circled around to follow him. He picked up a board of drywall sitting on a pile near the back door and I grabbed the other end. We worked our way with it into the kitchen and set it down.

"I don't think you have to worry. Sam seems like a really nice guy."

"Yeah, I know. I'm just a little protective."

"You do realize that's how she reacts to you dating Chelsea. She feels protective of you too."

"I think she's upset that I'm dating someone she doesn't approve of."

"Well, Chelsea and Aerie have a tough history. From what she said." Aerie had confided in me that Chelsea was her childhood bully. It was hard to get over that.

"Chelsea has changed a lot since then," Jay said.

I gave him a questioning look that he didn't notice because he was applying the adhesive to the wall studs. The girl did try to punch me in the face not too long ago. My guess was that she hadn't changed that much since they were younger.

"Can you take this end of the board and hold it up for me while I get the other end?"

"Sure." I followed his instruction.

Jay walked the wallboard to the corner and fit it in place, securing it with a quick motion from the nail gun. I could tell he had done this lots of times. He had an easy way about him as he moved through the motions of putting up the wall. I admired it. I had to stop myself from admiring it too much. He was taken. I didn't need the heartache of another relationship.

We went outside and picked up the next board. We worked this way through the next hour and a half. But my arms were tired, and my ribs screamed in protest. I accidentally let out a moan, which he clearly heard.

"Why don't we stop for something to drink?"

"Good idea. I've got some sodas in the dining room."

The dining room was where I kept my mini fridge and

cases of soda. Along with bags of random snack food. We walked to the front of the house and I let both of us in. I motioned for Jay to help himself to a soda, which he did but then he picked up one of those bags of junk food. "I'm surprised Aerie hasn't given you the third degree."

"I suppose one of the benefits of getting my kitchen back would be that I'll eat healthier foods."

"I do miss Aerie's cooking." Jay chuckled.

It was an inside joke. Aerie's idea of cooking was chopping raw vegetables, which is how I came to cook at the diner.

"I can cook for you, anytime you want." I was surprised at the subtle innuendo that my voice had put into that sentence. I blushed. Then again, I wasn't so surprised. Much as I tried to tamp down the crush, it was still there. Unfortunately, I think Jay noticed it.

"Well, look, it's been a long afternoon. I'll let you rest up." He gathered his tools.

A frantic pounding on my front door made us both jump. I rushed past Jay and pulled it open to find Aerie in tears. As soon as she saw me she grabbed me by the shoulders. "They think Sam did it."

"Did what?"

"They think Sam stole the crane." She looked past me and saw Jay and she lunged toward him. "Jay, you have to talk to Dan. Tell him he's crazy to think that Sam would do this. Can you please go down to the police station right now?"

Jay looked confused but nodded. "Yeah. Of course. I can go with you."

The three of us walked down the street toward the police station. To our surprise, when we got there, Sam appeared to be ready to leave. Detective Lockheart was shaking his hand. "Thanks for coming down, Sam. I'll be in touch."

Aerie immediately went to Sam, but I followed Jay, who was friends with Detective Lockheart. "Dan, what's going on?" Jay asked.

"We found the crane. It was in Harrisburg, some thirty miles away. And there is some evidence that points to Sam's involvement. Not enough to hold him, but he isn't to leave town. I can't say more than that."

"You can't believe that Sam is involved?" I said.

It looked as if Detective Lockheart had just noticed me. "What are you doing here?"

"It might surprise you, but I have friends, too," I announced.

The corner of his mouth turned up slightly. "Look, I can't talk about an ongoing investigation. But Sam is not under arrest and he can go."

"You know he had nothing to do with it." I hoped Detective Lockheart would feel the dagger I was shooting his way.

"Ms. Michaels. I hate to have to repeat myself, but I feel like I must. Do not get involved in this investigation."

"Have you looked into each of the workers?" It was obvious to me something was going on between the men at the site.

"Leave the detecting to the professionals." He raised a hand. "Stay away from this."

I put my hands on my hips. "Or what? You'll arrest me again?"

"Don't tempt me."

Jay hooked his arm through my elbow and walked me over toward Aerie and Sam, at the door.

Sam rubbed Aerie's back. "It's all fine. Dan says it's just a matter of procedure. He has to interview me."

"Why? What did they find?" Aerie looked up at Sam.

"Flour. Some of my flour was inside the cab of the crane." He shrugged it off.

"That's ridiculous. It must have been planted there. It's not like you leave trails of pizza flour everywhere you go." I felt like he was being framed.

"He has to investigate everything. I'm not under arrest." He turned. "I have to get back to the restaurant."

"I'll come with you." Aerie gave me a fleeting glance. Sam took her hand.

"Thanks, Aerie." He smiled.

Jay continued to talk to Dan, and I hung back a bit to see if I could hear their conversation. It appeared both were questioning Sam's innocence. I knew Jay was biased because Sam was dating his sister, but Dan? Well, if Dan wasn't going to be impartial it would be up to me to clear Sam's name.

Noah Weller pushed into the station like a hurricane. "Where is Detective Lockheart? I need to talk to him!"

I pointed in the direction of Jay and Dan.

"Detective Lockheart! I demand immediate action." He slammed his hand down on the reception counter.

"Let's relax, Mr. Weller. Tell me what is going on."

"You need to arrest that man."

"Slow down. What's happened?"

"The sign from the theater is now missing and that pizza man stole it!"

Detective Lockheart looked around at Jay and me. "If you'll excuse us?" He turned to Mr. Weller. "Sir, if you'll come with me so I can get a full statement."

Detective Lockheart led Mr. Weller toward the conference room.

Jay turned to me. "I'd like to go over to the plaza. Can you drive?"

"Sure." I was just as determined to find out what was going on as Jay was.

6

Jay wanted to talk to his friend Karl who was the general contractor on the site, and I decided to talk to the other owners in the plaza to see if anybody had seen anything.

I would work left to right across the plaza, Sam's being the last business before the construction area. I pulled up the list Aerie and I made when we sat in the parking lot during the rainstorm.

The Ace Hardware store was owned by a man named Bob Earl. I jammed my phone in my back pocket and headed into the store. I thought for a moment about what I could buy while I was here. I was pretty sure if I bought something it would make the owner a little more conversational. It couldn't hurt. A drywall sander? Putty knife?

Well, here goes. I pulled open the door and stepped inside. The shop was bright and spotlessly clean, and smelled slightly of lawn fertilizer and lilacs. A nicely placed display of John Deere lawn mowers sat at the center of the room. The green and yellow shined like racecars.

I stopped to check things out and get my bearings, looking for an office where the owner might be at the back of the store. An older gentleman in denim and a flannel shirt and quilted vest stepped out of an aisle in front of me.

"Good afternoon. How can I help you?"

"I'm actually looking for Bob."

"You've found him." He offered his hand. "How can I help?"

"Oh, hi. I'm doing some drywall," I blurted out as I shook his hand.

"Right this way." He walked toward the aisles on the left past the checkout counters. "Nice weather we're having lately."

"Yeah. Not too hot."

"Oh, it'll get hotter. Make sure you keep your lawn watered come July. We have sprinklers here." He pointed to the aisle as we passed. "Here we are, dry wall. What are you looking for exactly?"

"I'm actually helping a friend with it. Maybe a putty knife?"

"Sure, here are a number of putty knives." He pointed to two. "These two are more ergonomic, easier to hold if you're working for a long time."

"We're just doing one room."

"Then any one of these others would work for you. Do you need putty or sanders?"

"I think Jay will have those."

"Oh." He grinned. "You're working with Jay McIntyre? I know him well."

I couldn't help but smile back. This guy gave off a fatherly vibe. "He's been helping me fix my kitchen."

"Were you the one whose kitchen caught fire last month?"

"Unfortunately, yes."

Nothing like a small town where everyone will always know what's going on. Oddly, I didn't mind so much. I was getting used to it here. And if everyone knew everything, then someone would know enough about the missing crane to clear Sam's name.

He nodded solemnly. "House fires are always a shame. Anything you need, you let me know. I'll discount it for you."

"You don't have to do that."

"It's neighborly. I can't help build it with you, but I can help you fix it up."

I smiled at him and when I looked beyond his shoulder. I noticed kitchen appliances in the back. I had to remind myself that I was here to interview Bob about the missing items from the worksite, and not shopping.

"Bob? Do you know about the missing crane over at the other end of the plaza?"

"Oh, sure, hard not to."

"Did you happen to see anything out of the ordinary?" I angled myself away from the back so I couldn't see the professional-grade six-burner chef stove out of the corner of my eye.

"I can't say that I did. The contractors don't usually come in here. They get their supplies elsewhere. Although occasionally if they need a quick replacement, they will come in." He gave me an uncertain, distracted look.

"I'm asking because one of my friends Sam Andrews is being framed."

"Well, I have to tell you, the guys they hired are a motley crew. That group was obviously thrown together, probably on the cheap. I wouldn't be surprised if it was one of them that was up to no good."

"Really?"

"Thinking about it, I had some discrepancies with my inventory last week that I thought was a computer error. But...well, I'll keep my eyes on them if any of them come in again."

"Could you let me know what was missing?"

"Sure. Let me get my computer." He grabbed his laptop, put on some reading glasses, and pulled up a page. "Looks like bungee cords, a wrench set, a few carabiners. Pretty random stuff."

"Thanks, Bob." I would make a note of the items when I got back to the car. I glanced back at the oven, and gave in. "Could I take a look at the appliances?"

"Sure, come on back." He grinned.

MEETING BOB HAD BEEN PLEASANT. I had some ideas for my future kitchen appliances, and he promised to keep an eye out in the plaza for anything that would point to someone causing *malarkey* as he put it. I listed the items missing from his store on the second page in my notebook.

I felt a bit silly walking into the day spa with a putty knife in hand, so I took it to my car before heading into my next interview. I glanced over at the worksite as I popped my trunk. Jay stood talking to Karl. I couldn't wait to hear what he learned. I was really glad Jay was helping out with this even if he was biased against Sam. Facts were facts. Aerie was always great at working on these kinds of mysteries, and I missed her company while we figured things out. But she had a boyfriend now and I understood coming in second.

I entered the spa and was greeted by an excess of air-conditioned ambiance. The lighting here wasn't quite as bright as the hardware store, a subtle and calming difference.

"Hi, Mira!" Cara called from the back of the salon. Trying to quickly come up with something I could buy, I blurted, "Hi Cara. Can I get my nails done?"

"Gel, acrylics, or basic? We also have paraffin wax if you're interested. It's very relaxing."

Even though I wasn't still holding the putty knife, I knew drywalling was still in my future. Was I about to pay for something that was going to chip two seconds after I pick up the next drywall board? "Do you have anything super long-lasting and durable?"

"Acrylics are good for long lasting, but you cook at the diner, right? You might not want longer nails. Gel is harder to chip and it's easy to remove when you are bored with the color."

"Gel sounds good. Thanks."

"Let me get the table set up, you can choose from any of the colors along the wall."

The large rack attached to the wall of nail polish bottles was organized in a rainbow of color.

I decided to go with the teal. It reminded me of summer beach vacations. Something I could use right now. I took the bottle off the shelf and walked over to the table where Cara was setting up the various tools and nail files.

"That's a great color. Really popular right now."

"Thanks." After we settled into the comfy chairs, I dove right to the reason I was there. "Have you seen anything, in the parking lot or around the construction area, that seems suspicious to you?"

"What do you mean by suspicious?"

"First a popcorn machine was taken then a crane was stolen, now the sign for the theater is missing."

"She stopped filing my nails for a second and looked at me. "You're kidding?"

"Nope. Truth. I don't know who would want to steal the theater sign, popcorn machine maybe."

"Well, I suppose somebody doesn't want the theater to open up."

"I hadn't thought of that," I lied.

"Oh, yeah, I'm sure there were people who weren't too excited about an expansion of the plaza. There are always people against progress, I suppose."

"Oh, yeah, I guess so. Hey, thanks for the great haircut the other day, I really appreciate it. It feels so much lighter."

"You're welcome."

"Do you guys get a lot of business in the plaza?"

"A fair amount. Lots of repeat customers. Ilsa just started the spa treatments, which are a big hit."

"Oh, what kind of treatments?" I could desperately use one. My arms were still stiff from hanging the drywall with Jay.

"We offer different types of massage and therapies. One of the most popular is a couples massage therapy that we do in the evening."

"Oh, well, I'm not dating anybody."

"That doesn't mean you can't get a massage." She wiped my fingernails with acetone and started painting.

"Right now, a manicure is probably all I can afford."

"I hear that. But you can always splurge on your birthday."

"After putting appliances in the new kitchen, I don't think I'll have much money to splurge on for quite a while."

Cara nodded. "Appliances are not cheap."

"I'm thinking of buying them from Bob next door."

"Oh, Bob's a nice guy. He would give you a fair price."

"I know. He insisted on giving me a discount today when I was in there buying something small."

We chatted more about the town and the new ice cream options at the diner. We even compared pet stories. Cara has a chihuahua with an attitude that might just rival Arnold's.

"The teal nail polish looks great on your hands."

"Thanks, it looks awesome."

"You can put your hands under this dryer while I finish and close up. I'm ready to go home."

I realized it was time for me to call it a day too. I would have to do the rest of the interviews tomorrow. I hoped Jay got some good information from Karl.

7

I met Jay in the parking lot near my car.

"Hey Mira, how did it go?" He looked down at my hands. "Nice nails."

I felt the blush rising up my neck to my cheeks. "Thanks. Hazard of the job. I was able to get some information from Bob at the hardware store too."

"Yeah? What has Bob seen?" Jay asked.

"He's missing some inventory, small stuff but didn't think much of it at the time beyond annoyance until he heard about the crane theft and now the sign."

"Yeah? What kind of stuff?"

"Let's see, he told me some bungee cords, a wrench set, and some carabiners. He also mentioned he doesn't really trust any of the workers. Bad vibe, he says."

"I got something similar from Karl, he calls the crew the desperadoes. He says Weller put together the crew because he's low on cash."

"That might be why he was so frantic at the police station."

"Karl is pretty sure Weller will go bankrupt if the

theater doesn't open on time. Weller needs to make a profit fast."

"But the desperadoes need the cash from the job. That would keep them out of the pool of suspects, they wouldn't want to stop the work, or they won't get paid."

Jay sat there for a moment. "Unless..."

"Unless what?"

"If the guys are really desperate for money there could be two ways to get more. Make the job last longer or steal the crane and sell it on the black market."

"Or both."

"Or both."

"Okay, so that means we have four people on the suspect list. Our desperadoes."

"I wouldn't put Karl on that list. He has a family that he's trying to support so I highly doubt that he would resort to stealing to do that."

"You did say he is going through a nasty divorce. Does he have some expensive alimony to pay?"

Jay gave me a look. "You can take him off the suspect list. I've known Karl a long time and he's a good guy."

"But you still think Sam might have done it?"

"It's possible."

"I think Sam has a lot more to lose if this theater doesn't go through. He can make a lot more money if the theater is up and running."

"Yeah. Maybe. Still, I don't trust him."

I put my hands on my hips. "Are you sure that's not just because your sister is dating him?"

"I am just being extra cautious."

"Remember that's what Aerie is doing with you and Chelsea."

"She doesn't need to worry about me."

I gave Jay the side-eye that he ignored, so I grumbled a bit. "Let's go get Aerie."

Aerie was sitting on the counter swinging her legs, talking quietly with Sam.

"Hey, Aerie, Jay and I were about to go, and we were wondering if you want a ride."

"Sure." She jumped down from the counter. "I'll see you a bit later," she told Sam.

I grinned almost apologetically at Sam, who still looked upset about the turn of events.

Once we got to the car, I asked Jay and Aerie, "Ready for dinner? My place or yours?"

"Sorry Mira, I'm going out to dinner with Sam."

"Oh, okay," I said. "I can make myself a peanut butter sandwich, no problem."

"Whoa. Wait a minute." Jay turned in his seat awkwardly to face Aerie. "Aren't you rushing it a bit?"

"What are you talking about?" She snapped.

"Maybe you should wait until after we find out what's going on."

"Do you think Sam did this?" In the rearview I saw Aerie narrow her eyes at her brother.

"Maybe. You don't know for sure that he's innocent." Jay faced front.

"Well, I know he's innocent. He didn't do this."

"I'm heading back to the house." I tried to buffer the volleys between siblings.

"I'm just saying that maybe it would be better…"

"You don't want me dating Sam, is that it?" Aerie screeched out.

"No, I think you should just wait." He said it so matter-of-factly even my blood pressure went up.

"You are so hypocritical! You got all up in my face when I

told you not to date Chelsea. And I *had* a reason. She bullied me for years."

"I didn't say you can't date Sam. I'm just saying don't date him right now." He heavily emphasized "now".

"He didn't do this. And it's more than insulting that you think he could. And I'm even more insulted that you would question my own judgment."

"Like you question mine?" Jay's voice rose.

"She was a bully. She ruined my life for years."

"She's a different person now." His response was quieter.

"I'll believe that when I see it." Aerie said with an exasperated sigh. "And I can date whomever I want, Jay. I'm a grown woman."

"Then act like it. Wait until the investigation is over."

"I can't even stand you right now. Mira, drive faster. I want out of this car."

"I'm driving as fast as I legally can." I wanted to get out of this car, too.

The remainder of the ride was deadly silent. When I pulled up to Aerie and Jay's house, Aerie hopped out and slammed the door without looking back.

Jay cleared his throat. "Can you just drive me to the worksite, so I can pick up my truck?"

"Miller's barn, right?"

"Yeah. It's down Main Street, hang a left on Oak. Then take that for a couple miles."

"Will do."

Jay and I didn't talk as we drove out to Miller's barn. I didn't blame him for wanting Aerie to wait on dating Sam. But at the same time, I didn't feel that Sam had enough of a motive and really felt that for some reason, someone was framing him. Besides, I knew Aerie; she would do whatever she wanted to do. No matter what Jay said.

By the time we got to the work site it was dark. But some really bright lights were focused on the new shed that was going up.

"You guys work in the dark?" I asked.

"With lights. Mr. Miller needs the shed done tonight. He has a shipment of chicks coming in tomorrow."

"Chicks?"

"Yeah, Mr. Miller raises layer hens. Where do you think your organic cage-free eggs come from?"

"Oh, cool." I looked at the large shed and wondered out loud. "How many chicks is he getting?"

"I don't know, I think 500."

"Wow, that's a lot of eggs."

Jay got out of the car but leaned down to peer through the window. "I know Aerie is mad with me right now, but can you do me a favor and keep an eye on her and Sam?"

"You know I will." Actually, I planned to figure out the mystery of the missing crane.

"I want to keep looking into this. Will you help me?"

"Of course. I want to find out who did this just as much as you do."

"Good. Hey, thanks for the ride."

"No problem." I drove around the circular drive and headed back home. Jay and Aerie had a solid sibling rivalry going on right now. It almost made me nostalgic for Darla. Almost.

SUNDAY MORNING at the diner was a busy one. Mrs. Orsa didn't even try to chat with us like she usually did. She just paid her bill and gave me a sweet smile when I waved to her. "Have a good morning, Mrs. Orsa."

"You girls make sure you take a break today."

"Will do. See you tomorrow, Mrs. Orsa," Aerie called to her while bussing a table.

We had a slight lull around nine-thirty. Aerie showed up in the kitchen. "I have a huge favor to ask."

I flipped sets of the half-dollar pancakes with my offset spatula. "Sure. What's up?"

"Sam invited me to go on a date."

"Oh really?" This was an exciting new announcement. Although I had expected it.

"Yeah, he wants to take me out to lunch and walk around the Canyon."

"So, you'd like to leave soon?"

"Yeah. But we're so busy. I can stay. He and I can make a date another day."

"Sam is going to close up his shop?"

"No, he'll let Scott run it. He called it 'trial by fire'."

"Well, no reason you couldn't do that for me. I really don't mind. Although we could get Jay if he's not working today."

A series of emotions played across Aerie's face. She wasn't sure she could ask him.

"He does still own half of the diner," I reminded her. "You should put him to work."

"I don't know."

"You just don't want to hear what he has to say about Sam."

"Nope."

"I'll ask him. Don't worry about it. Go on your date."

"Really? You'll be okay?"

"I'll get Jay. It will be fine. Go on your date."

Aerie's eyes lit up and she lunged and hugged me even though I had a spatula full of pancakes.

"Is it okay if I leave at ten-thirty?"

"Of course. Have fun, okay?"

"Thanks. I owe you one."

"No, you don't." She had supported me everyday since I got to this town. Running the diner today, even as busy as it was, was the least I could do.

She hurried out to the dining room to help as new customers arrived.

I plated the orders that were ready and pulled out my cell phone to call Jay. "Hey, Jay?"

"Yeah, what's up? Did you find out something?"

"Not yet. But I'm wondering if you can come and help me at the diner in about an hour."

"What happened? Where is Aerie?"

"Everything is fine. She just has a date with Sam. But today is super busy and I could really use the help."

"Yeah. Hold on a sec." I heard some muffled arguing on the other end of the phone line and pretended not to eavesdrop. I couldn't hear enough to understand anyway.

"Yeah, yeah, I can come in. I'll see you in about an hour." He hung up without waiting for a reply.

I jammed my cell phone into my back pocket. Jay had to figure out his domestic issues on his own. "Good luck with that," I mumbled under my breath.

The back door to the kitchen was open to let in some cooler air and I fanned some in my direction. The grill was hot.

About forty-five minutes later, Jay's truck rumbled down Main Street, and within seconds, Aerie had whipped off her apron and rushed through the kitchen. "See ya."

"Chicken."

"Cluck, cluck. If he can't see me, he can't complain."

"Have fun!" I shouted as she ducked out the kitchen door.

At the same moment, the entrance door chimed. Diners greeted Jay as he came in.

"Long time, no see."

"When was the last time you set foot in here?" Mike from the post office ribbed him.

"Good to see you." The voice that traveled to the kitchen was Detective Lockheart's and I grimaced. Why did he always have to have lunch here?

"Hey, Mira." Jay's deep voice resounded in the small kitchen space.

I was scraping off the grill, trying not to look as hot and tired as I already felt.

"Thanks for coming Jay, I appreciate it." I wiped my hand across my forehead and hoped my hair wasn't sticking up.

"Where's Aerie?" Jay glanced about the kitchen.

I just grinned. "On her date, I expect."

Jay grumbled and put the apron on over his head. "I can cook." He peered closer at my face. "You have a little..." he reached over. His thumb brushed my cheek. Instinctively I reached up to my face and our hands smashed into each other. I half giggled with embarrassment and changed the subject. "You? You can cook?"

"Our parents had me cooking on that very grill since I was fourteen. I think I can manage to not burn the place down." As soon as he said it, he cringed. The first few weeks of me cooking here led to a visit by the volunteer fire department. He looked so remorseful I blurted out a laugh.

"Don't worry about it. I'm over it. You sure you want to cook? It gets hot in here."

"Can't stand the heat, get out of the kitchen?"

"There's a reason they say it."

"I can handle it." Jay checked the white board like a seasoned pro and prepped the items he'd need.

Then I remembered Detective Lockheart was out at the counter. "Can we wait until a certain police figure is finished with his meal and has left the building?"

"Are you chicken?"

"Funny. Irony. That's funny," I said to myself.

"What?"

"Nothing. The universe is laughing at me right now, that's all." I took off my grill apron and grabbed Aerie's with the marker and board in the pocket. I squared my shoulders, took a deep breath, and headed out to the dining room.

"Hello, Detective Lockheart," I said evenly.

"Ms. Michaels." He raised his menu. "You're letting Jay cook?"

"Sure. Why not?" Detective Lockheart and Jay were close friends. Obviously, there was some backstory here that I was missing.

"Oh, no reason. Tell him I don't want frog."

"Ew." I held up my hand. "I don't want to know."

He grinned at his own inside joke, went back to his phone, and I began the rounds at each table.

Since the lunch crowd was spread out between eleven and two, the lunch hours weren't quite as intense as breakfast had been. But Dan remained at the counter taking a very leisurely time finishing off his lunch, again a hamburger, not a frog. I just knew that at any moment he would reprimand me about doing any kind of research into the thefts at the worksite. I just knew it. But the longer I waited the less inclined he appeared to be to say anything to me. What was he up to? Finally, my nerves got the better of me.

"Why exactly are you still here?"

He paused for a moment. "I was thinking about whether or not I should have an ice cream cone or an ice cream sundae."

It took me a moment to register what he said, and that it had nothing to do with investigating any case.

"You want ice cream?" I still didn't believe him.

"I'm pretty sure that's what I just said." He grinned. When he smiled like that he was startlingly handsome. Which immediately made me angry. He wasn't supposed be good-looking and so annoying.

"Okay then, what flavor do you want?"

"I heard talk of some new flavor, chocolate raspberry?"

"Who told you? Oh, never mind. Do you want a cone or sundae?"

"That's what I was hoping you could help me out with."

I looked at him sideways. What was he up to? Was he trying to get me to spill information? "What do you mean? Do you want to know the difference in cost?"

"No. Will I enjoy the cone or the sundae more?" He infuriatingly smiled again.

"What kind of question is that?"

"A simple one. But I see I'm not getting anywhere. I'll take a small cone please."

I stepped to the cabinet, took down a sugar cone and headed to the freezer. I scooped a decent amount of ice cream and pushed it gently into the cone. I even rounded the top slightly. I took out a paper napkin, a concession I made with Aerie. The small use of paper napkins would save a lot more than washing ice cream laden cloth ones.

I handed the ice cream to Detective Lockheart. "Here you go."

"Thanks." He took the cone and as he licked the ice cream, I had to force myself to look away.

That was it. That was all he said.

I just stood there waiting for him to say something. When he was halfway through his cone, he stopped and looked at me.

"I'm okay with you investigating," he said.

"What?" I had to be hearing things.

"I know you've been talking to people." He was so calm.

"You do? I mean..." I fumbled with my apron. "I don't know what you're talking about." I turned to hide in the kitchen.

"You don't have to pretend. I've come to understand that you're going to investigate any issue that comes up in this town. It warms the heart."

"Warms the heart?"

"I'm telling you, I don't mind that you do your own investigation as long as it doesn't interfere with mine."

"Oh, I see. As long as I don't interfere." I stressed the last word.

"You do seem to find out information that I can't obtain through my investigative techniques. I won't say that it hasn't helped in the past."

"Yeah, I solved your cases for you." He knew that even if he didn't want to admit it.

"Well, I don't know about that..."

"But I have."

He smiled. "Did I mention I like the ice cream?"

I WAS STILL MUSING about what happened to Detective Lockheart to bring on his new attitude about me investigating, until long after Jay and I closed the diner. I felt oddly self-conscious about investigating now. Wait. Was that his plan all along? To make me second-guess myself so I wouldn't investigate?

Well, I wouldn't let him stop me. There was one shop I hadn't been into along the strip mall—the Pocket Moon Pottery shop.

THE POTTERY SHOP was bright and inviting. Front and center sat a display of brightly colored and decorated plates, bowls, and mugs. To the left was a series of tables all set up for a picnic, but with paintbrushes instead of silverware, mason jars of water instead of drinks, and paper plates for mixing paints instead of food.

Along the back walls were pieces of stark white pottery. The sound of children giggling and playing echoed from somewhere in the back of the shop.

"Hello, can I help you?" A checkout counter was to my immediate right and a woman in a leather biker jacket leaned over it toward me. "We're open, you can help yourself to the piece you'd like to paint. Any table is fine, paints are along the walls." She pointed to the back wall where a shelf full of small round hockey puck shaped disks held a rainbow of paints.

"I'm actually wondering if I can ask you a few questions," I said.

The woman walked out from behind the counter. Under the jacket she wore a baby-doll dress and iridescent lilac Doc Martins. I immediately liked her.

"Sure, what can I help you with?"

"Hi. I'm Mira Michaels." I shook her hand.

"I'm Heather Gerry, the owner."

"I'm actually wondering if you have seen anything over at the work site for the theater."

"Oh?"

"There have been some thefts and I'm just asking around if anyone had seen anything unusual."

A woman stepped out from a room in the back looking concerned.

Ms. Gerry held up her hand. "The three o'clock birthday party is starting. Let me get that situated. I might be a few minutes."

"No problem. Is it okay if I just look around?"

"Help yourself." She disappeared into the back, obviously to help with the birthday party and set the parent's mind at ease.

I walked around the shop. I noticed a set of windows behind the counter that looked out onto the parking lot. I stepped behind the counter. The checkout desk had a basic computer and printer set up. The windows were the most interesting. While looking out onto a parking lot is not usually the best view, in this case, it had a perfect view of the work site. I imagined that if Ms. Gerry sat here all day, she would have a fine view of anything that happened. Like a giant crane being stolen, a theater sign or a walking popcorn maker.

I wandered back out to look around the shelves at potential creative projects. A signup sheet hung on the wall for GNO - BYOB - Thursdays. Girls Night Out. Bring Your Own Bottle. Hmm. I'd have to ask Aerie if she'd like to do it. Maybe not now that she was in a new relationship. I remembered the magic of a new relationship. Mine just always went south soon after that honeymoon phase. She wouldn't want to hang out with me, at least not for a little while. I sighed. I tried to switch gears and remind myself: I'm a rolling stone; I'm just going to flip this house and leave. But this town had pulled me in. I was a part of it now and I liked it. Its quirkiness fit my quirkiness.

My phone buzzed. It was my sister, calling instead of texting. We had set up an agreement that for all sisterly advice she would text, but if she had a hunch about anything dangerous again, she'd call, and I had promised her I would pick up the phone. So, it was understandable that the bottom of my stomach felt like it was in free fall. I walked over to the shelves of ceramics.

I pushed the answer button. "What?" I snapped.

"Hello is usually a more congenial way to answer the phone." Her voice intoned older sister reprimand which turned my fear into frustration.

"I know that. But you're calling so that must mean it's something dangerous, right?"

"Well..."

"You swore you would only call if you had a vision about something dangerous. You promised you wouldn't call anymore just to let me know how much I'm messing up my life."

"You're never messing up your life. You're just making uninformed decisions."

"Thank you, yes. Uninformed. And you promised me you would stop trying to inform those decisions." I ran my hand over a ceramic elephant.

"I did."

There was silence on the other end of the phone for about two seconds too long. "And?" I asked.

"I had a vision about a lot of water."

"That's it?"

"Yes. But it was very dangerous."

"Darla!"

"Look, it had all the danger symbols, so it wasn't subtle. There's going to be a great deal of dangerous water in your future."

"Well, what am I supposed to do about that?"

"Stay away from water."

"Seriously Darla? Are you telling me not to shower or wash the dishes or what?" I picked up a white mug. I could use some new dishes.

"Just be very careful around it then. Anything where there's a lot of water in one place."

"You are so frustrating."

"You should try being a psychic."

"I gotta go and pretend my life is normal."

"Good luck with that." She chuckled.

"Thanks."

"Mira?" Her voice held a level of concern that did make my stomach drop. "Be careful."

I punched the end call button with all the force I could muster without poking my phone to the floor and jammed it in my back pocket.

Thankfully at that moment Ms. Gerry came out of the birthday room and headed in my direction. "Everyone is busy painting."

"Oh, that's good." I pointed to the window behind the counter. "You have a good view of the work site."

"I suppose you could call it that. Not much to see, really."

"Anything you would call out of the ordinary?"

She thought for a moment. "Not anything I can think of offhand."

I nodded. "Okay. Well, if you see anything or remember anything can you give me a call?"

"Sorry, what was your name again?"

"Mira Michaels." I smiled and decided to run with it. After all, a certain detective said he was fine with me investigating. "I'm working with Detective Lockheart on the thefts."

She added my details into her cell phone, and I thanked her.

I wondered how many birthday parties she officiated and how often she got to sit and look out that window.

I thanked her. Out that same window, a white van pulled up to the work site. Karl walked briskly to it and shook the guy's hand through the open driver's window, but his body language screamed that he wasn't happy to see him.

8
_____

Of course, I wanted to find out what this meeting was about, so I left the pottery place and jogged quickly across the parking lot to the front of Sam's and pretended to go inside. Instead, I ducked behind some stacked drywall next to a ladder.

Karl, and the man whose name I didn't know, exchanged pleasantries as they entered the theater. The man had a clipboard with pen and paper and some kind of ID tag clipped to his shirt. When I finally got a look at it, it said, OSHA.

I vaguely remembered that OSHA had something to do with safety. Which would explain Karl's anxiety. If there were any safety violations here, this guy could shut down construction.

I followed as closely behind as I could without being seen. Luckily they had their backs to me when I opened the door. Utilizing all the piles of construction materials and hoping my sandals wouldn't squeak on the floor, I ended up next to another ladder and a pile of drywall, cables, and miscellaneous materials. Right beyond the ladder was a giant fish tank with two huge koi fish. One orange, the other a cool shade of blue. I guessed it would be for people to watch while they waited in line for popcorn. Fancy. I had never been in a movie theater that had a fish tank. Why would he have live fish here in a work zone?

The OSHA guy was slow and methodical. I desperately wanted to duck out. But this information could be important to solving the case. Especially if someone was framing Sam. So, I crept along behind them.

"You see this right here?" The OSHA guy pointed at a ladder propped against the wall. "This is a hazard." He marked something on the clipboard.

"I'll have it taken care of immediately."

The OSHA man nodded. "I prefer to do the rest of the inspection on my own, if you don't mind. I'll come back and let you know what I find."

"Of course. I'll wait here." Karl looked more nervous than ever.

The OSHA man continued to inspect the area. I sat in my hiding space and waited.

After what felt like a million years, the OSHA man circled back to address Karl. "You have a fall protection violation in the northwest corner. And you have some improperly grounded electrical systems. This needs to be taken care of immediately."

"Improperly grounded electrical? I'll have it looked at ASAP."

"Once you have that completed and up to code, you can contact me at this number, and I'll come back and re-inspect. Until that time, all construction must stop. I'll inform the owner via email." He tucked the clipboard under his arm and reached out to shake Karl's hand. "Thank you for your time today. I'll await your phone call."

Karl stood there, dumbfounded. I tried to get a closer look and tripped on one of the electrical cords, banging my hip on the fan. Trying to untangle my foot quietly was impossible. I stepped on the cord with my other foot to pin it in place and ended up tripping over the cable that was now wrapped around my ankle. I refused to sprain something this time. I had to pull the cable to get free, but it seemed stuck around the legs of the ladder. The more I tugged, the more the ladder wobbled and tilted. I stopped mid-breath. Too late. The OSHA guy strode over. A sound caught my attention. I looked up. The paint cans teetered at the top of the ladder. Just as the OSHA man stepped next to me, I closed my eyes and held my breath. An ocean of Tawny Tan poured down over both of us. With my eyes shut I heard the hollow sound of that second can of paint as it clocked the OSHA guy on the noggin.

AFTER EXTRICATING myself from that situation and enduring an embarrassing talking-to by the inspector and getting Karl in even more trouble for having a non-employee on the worksite, I found an unfinished bathroom and washed off as much of the paint as possible, then headed back to the parking lot, dripping water mixed with the bit of paint I hadn't managed to wash off. At this moment I felt my best option was to go home and hide under a rock.

I was consoling myself that it could have been worse. I could have shattered the giant fish tank. Maybe that was the water Darla was talking about?

As I passed Sam's, Aerie darted out and grabbed my wrist. "I need you to come with me right now." She looked anxious and then paused. "Why are you all wet?"

"Never mind. What's going on?" I followed her into The Pizza Pub. "Is everything all right?" The idea of water and danger flashed through my mind. Ugh, my sister. I was probably going to be thinking about dangerous water for the rest of the week.

She took me by the shoulders. "If I tell you something you have to swear to me you won't tell anybody else."

"Sure. I won't say anything. What is it?"

"Come with me." She tugged my arm. I followed her past customers enjoying their late lunches into the pizza kitchen. I wondered if any of them had heard the kerfuffle from the ladder and paint cans falling over next door.

Sam leaned heavily against the prep counter. He didn't glance up when I entered.

I looked at Aerie. "What's going on?"

"We found this near the kitchen door this morning." Aerie held up a plastic zip-top bag.

I squinted and held it closer. Inside was a piece of red plastic, about the size of a playing card. "What is it?" I asked even though I had a sinking suspicion.

"It's part of the theater sign."

"And you found it here?" I scanned the kitchen.

"Yes, obviously, somebody's trying to frame Sam."

I turned it over inside the bag. "We should give it to Detective Lockheart to check for fingerprints."

"He'll arrest Sam. He already doesn't like him."

"What do you mean he doesn't like him?"

"Sam and Dan have bad blood."

Sam cleared his throat. "We don't need to talk about it. Dan doesn't like me. He's going to arrest me if he sees this plastic."

"What do you want me to do about it?" I asked.

Aerie took my hand. "We want you to keep this with you,

79

if Dan finds it here... Can you please help us solve who is trying to frame Sam? Maybe later when we know who it is we can give this to Dan, but not now."

"I don't know, Aerie." Warning bells were clanging in my mind.

"You never had a problem hiding stuff from Dan before." Her voice was laced with the slightest bit of anger.

"Yeah, but..." I thought about this morning when Dan trusted me to share my information and be a responsible investigator. Hiding this would crush that trust.

Why did I care? But I did.

Still, Aerie was right. If he found this Dan would arrest Sam, at least until he figured out what was going on.

"Okay, I'll take it." This was so against my better judgment. But my loyalty was with Aerie. And that transferred to her new boyfriend. I had to solve this mystery before Detective Dan ever learned I had this thing.

9

You smell like paint.

Arnold sat across from me next to the doggy toy bin where I stuffed the broken piece of plastic.

"I've showered. I can't possibly smell like paint." Arnold could be so annoying.

Why are you putting trash in Ozzy's toy bin? Not that I care.

"It's not trash, it's evidence. I might need it later." Why was I even explaining this to him? Maybe my guilty conscience needed the support.

Arnold nodded. *Yes, I hide things too, for later.* He stalked off toward the sunny spot in the living room.

I stared at his sleek black furry body for a moment. Nope, I wouldn't take the bait. I did not want to know what he was hiding. I only hoped it wasn't something that would smell later.

I wanted to know more about what happened with Karl and the OSHA guy. I told Aerie I planned to hang out at my house and maybe help Jay finish hanging the drywall. I wanted to ask him what it meant to fail the inspection. But I didn't want to tell him that I had been eavesdropping or the end result of said eavesdropping. I was still trying to get Tawny Tan out of my hair.

Jay's truck pulled up at 9 a.m. on the dot. I went outside to greet him. I knew from the huge grin on his face that he had heard what happened at the theater.

"I expected to see you with a new hair color." Jay stifled a laugh.

"Ha, ha. Very funny. You heard?" I assumed Karl had told him.

"It's hard not to hear about the crazy antics that you get up to. How exactly did you get the paint to pour all over the OSHA inspector?"

"I didn't mean to knock the paint over. I was trying to get untangled from an electrical cable. That guy just happened to be there." I groused.

He nodded sagely. "Karl wasn't sure if he should laugh or cry."

"I made it worse for him, didn't I?" I felt badly.

"Well, it didn't make it better." Jay shrugged.

"Can you tell him I'm sorry?"

Jay shook his head. "He has his own issues he has to deal with on that worksite. I don't envy him."

"The inspector said he had to shut down everything until he fixes the problems, right?"

"Yeah, he has to bring in an electrician to double check that the system is grounded properly."

"Does that take a long time?"

"It can, if the original electrician isn't available." He shook his head like he knew that would be a task.

"Do you think he'll be back to work by the end of the week?" I wanted to give Aerie and Sam some good news.

"Maybe. Karl's going to try his best, because from what

he says, the owner, Weller, is a nervous wreck about the opening. Especially now that the sign has gone missing."

I almost choked. "I heard about that."

Who would want the theater to close so badly? And who would even think to frame Sam? He was such a nice guy. I had to figure this out. The last thing I wanted was for Sam to end up being interviewed by Dan again. Jay had a hard enough time with Aerie dating someone. That poor someone had an uphill battle if he was also being interrogated by the police.

Jay brought out his drywall tools. Which included a squirt gun of adhesive, which reminded me of taffy and still cracked me up. We had our own method of hanging drywall. We made a good team. Still, I couldn't shake the feeling that I had to make a decision about the piece of the theater sign that I had hidden in the doggy toy bin in the next room.

What was I supposed to do about it? Was I just supposed to hold onto this thing until we figured out all the answers? I replayed the conversation I had with Detective Lockheart in my head. He trusted me to do a good investigation. Even I knew holding onto evidence was not good investigating.

"You're quiet today."

"Sorry." Jay shook me out of my ruminations. "Just thinking."

"Are you trying to figure out whodunnit?"

I had to chuckle at that. "Is it that obvious?"

Jay shrugged. "Whenever there's a mystery you seem connected to it like a magnet." He nailed in the board we were working on.

"I don't know if I should take that as a compliment or what."

"A compliment for sure. You always seem to solve the problem. And that's admirable." He smiled at me.

"Admirable? I don't think I've ever been called admirable before." I stood back to enjoy Jay's handiwork. The kitchen was looking more like a room again, and less like a burned-out cave.

"Do you think you'll be able to solve it?" He stepped back with me.

"Who is responsible for trying to shut down the opening of the theater?"

"It's pretty obvious somebody has it out for that worksite. Karl is looking at this job as a comedy of errors."

"That bad?" Things were piling up. The popcorn machine, the crane, the sign.

"He's had problems since the very beginning. His crew is a mess. The owner is a nervous wreck. Now the worksite is falling apart. And he's trying to keep it all together."

"Uphill battle?"

"The spilled paint and the OSHA visit didn't help."

"Ugh."

"But don't let me stop you. Keep thinking it out in your head. I won't interrupt. Maybe you can solve this problem for Karl and everybody else involved."

"That would be great if—poof—the solution would just show up out of the blue." And then I thought of my sister and how often that happens for her.

True to his word, Jay worked in silence giving me minimal direction on helping him hold up the drywall.

I surprised myself at how difficult it was for me to keep this piece of evidence and not to tell Detective Lockheart. I shook my head. He said he trusted me. And I thought that was the linchpin. Right then and there I decided I would give Detective Lockheart the evidence. I just had to figure out a way to tell him how I came about having the piece of the sign without incriminating Sam or Aerie.

Jay finished the board we were working on. "Hey, I forgot to mention that the door you ordered for the kitchen is on back order."

"Oh, really?" I was disappointed. "I was looking forward to being able to take down the plywood."

"I would keep it up. It's safer that way. I know we're a small town, but you don't want to leave your house open like that. Just wait. We'll get the door, and once it's installed, I'll help you take down that plywood."

"Will you bring a big sledgehammer?"

"Only a small hammer will be necessary. I just need to pull out the nails." Then he smiled. "I get it. You want to smash something? Remind me to take you to the next house remodel when we start the demo. Then you can really smash some stuff."

"That sounds like a plan. Thanks again, Jay. I really appreciate your help with all of this." I walked around the middle of the room, which now really felt like a room. With Bob's help at the hardware store, I might actually be able to afford at least the stove for starters.

"Not a problem. I had fun hanging drywall with you. Even if it was quiet."

"Sorry."

"No worries. I know you're busy solving a case."

"I don't know about that. But I'll try." Right now I didn't feel like much of a proper investigator.

"I have faith you'll figure it out." He grinned, another infuriating grin that melted my insides.

THIS WAS the fifth time I walked past the post office near the police station. I changed my mind five times. Detective Lockheart's voice kept repeating in my brain: "I trust you to do good investigating."

Holding on to this piece of evidence wasn't good investigating, I told myself. But then, the whole reason Aerie gave it to me was that it was specifically designed to frame Sam. Would Detective Lockheart see past that? I doubted it, and that's when I would turn to walk home.

But then I stared at the little piece of the sign again and realized that only Detective Lockheart had the equipment to test it for fingerprints. And sure, it would have Sam's fingerprints. Maybe Aerie's too. But it might also have the actual thief's fingerprints. Then we could end this whole investigation. Which was why I stood in front of the post office again for the fifth time right across the alleyway from the police station. All I had to do was cross over to the sidewalk.

Before I could change my mind yet again, I took a deep breath, walked across and opened the police station's entrance door. The air conditioning sent a shiver down my spine. And for two seconds I thought about turning around...until a voice stopped me.

"Ms. Michaels." It was detective Dan. I was committed now.

"Detective Lockheart." I forced a smile on my face.

"What brings you here today? Have you found out any interesting information about our theft?"

"As a matter of fact." I couldn't back out now.

His smile turned serious. "Let's go into my office." He escorted me to a small cubicle with a door.

"What have you found?"

I pulled the zip-top bag from my back pocket.

His handsome face darkened. "Where did you find that?" His question was remonstrative.

"Can you test it for fingerprints?" Because if he couldn't I was going to be in some hot water with Aerie.

"I asked you, where did you get this?" He took the bag from me and examined it.

"Look, I wasn't going to give this to you, but I realized that you have the equipment to find fingerprints on this thing. Can you?"

He held up the bag. "This is tampering with evidence."

"Don't get all angry with me. I'm sharing evidence with you. Evidence that you wouldn't have gotten ahold of otherwise."

I could see him think about that for a moment. "Whoever gave you this is incriminating themselves in the theft. So, I'm going to ask you again. Who gave this to you?"

"I can't tell you."

"What do you mean you can't tell me? This is an official investigation. I can put you in jail for withholding information."

"That's always your answer, isn't it? Put people under your thumb and force them to do your bidding."

"When it comes to the law, yes."

"I'm not telling you who gave that to me. I just want you to test it for fingerprints."

"I shouldn't have told you it was okay to investigate this. I should have known better. I should have known that you would get in the way."

"Get in the way? That's what you see me as—someone that gets in the way?" I took a step closer. "Do I need to remind you that I've helped you to solve the last two cases that you had? And that without me, you wouldn't have?"

"I would have solved the crimes. Without you. I'm a detective. That is what I do."

"That and threaten to throw people in jail for no good reason?"

"It's a good reason all right. Stop interfering with the investigation right now. I should never have said anything to you about helping. I regret it."

"Regret, huh? We'll see about regret." I turned on my heel and stormed toward the door.

"Is that a threat, Ms. Michaels?"

"Take it however you want to, Detective Lockheart. I'm out of here."

I couldn't hear if he followed me out, the blood of anger rushed through my ears. I heard nothing until I got to the diner. I pushed the door open and walked straight back to the kitchen.

10

S am had made us a full-fledged Italian dinner with
spaghetti, meatballs, cheesy garlic bread and tiramisu.
But the entire dinner had been quiet and reserved. The
elephant in the room was a piece of theater sign. Neither
Aerie nor Sam had asked me what I had done with it, and I
didn't tell them. I just hoped Detective Lockheart would be
able to find fingerprints on it that would shut down this case
against Sam.

I couldn't stand the silence any longer. "That was the
best dinner I've had in a long time. You guys will have to roll
me out of here." I gave a coarse laugh.

"Sam is an excellent cook." Aerie looked at him with
pride.

"Should I be worried about my job?" This time I really
laughed.

"I don't think so, Mira. If the theater goes in, I'll have
plenty of business right here.

"When it opens," Aerie corrected him, touching his arm
and smiling at him.

I felt like I was intruding, but then Aerie pulled her eyes

from Sam and grinned at me. "Thank you for helping with all of this..." She waved her hand around the words that even I couldn't find to describe the situation we were in.

The door opened. Suddenly Sam's face went pale. I twisted around in my seat as Detective Lockheart stepped into The Pizza Pub. I could tell by the look on his face that this wasn't good.

"Sam Andrews?" Detective Lockheart said.

Sam pushed back his chair and stood up.

"I'd like to take you down to the station and ask you a few more questions."

"I thought I had answered everything, Detective."

"New evidence has caused some questions to come up." His words were clipped and to the point.

"Right now?" Sam pointed out that we were still the middle of dinner.

"Please." Detective Lockheart motioned for Sam to step away from the table.

I stood up between Sam and Detective Lockheart. "What are you doing?"

"I'm taking Sam into the station for questioning."

This felt like Detective Lockheart's power play. "You don't need to take him away from his dinner for questioning."

"I'll be the judge of that. You didn't think I couldn't put two and two together and realize you must've gotten this from Sam." I closed my eyes as Detective Lockheart held up the piece of sign, now in an evidence bag. It was my turn for the color to drain from my face. And I felt Aerie shift behind me. Great. Now she thinks I've betrayed her.

"Someone is trying to frame Sam. You were supposed to find out who that is from that piece of evidence. Not come in here and arrest Sam." I was shouting now I was so furious.

"I'm not arresting Sam, I'm questioning him. And you need to stay out of this investigation from now on."

"You said... But again, you're obviously not doing your job. Because someone is trying to frame Sam and here you are taking him into custody."

"I am not taking Sam into custody, I'm simply asking him questions."

"At the station." I pointed out.

Detective Lockheart turned away from me and toward Sam. "Sam, if you wouldn't mind." He waved his hand toward the door.

Sam dropped his napkin on the table. "Scott, you lock up?"

"No problem, Sam," Scott said quietly.

I stood watching as Sam and Detective Lockheart had left. Aerie said nothing, refusing to look at me. She stormed out the door. I watched as she followed Detective Lockheart's car to the police station. I looked over at Scott, but he avoided my eyes as well. Well, fine. "Everyone hates me now." I sighed. I walked over to the counter, left $40 on it to pay for the meal and left.

KNOWING that both Sam and Aerie were now going to hate me forever didn't make entering the police station any easier. What did help was picking up Jay on the way over to the station.

"I screwed up. I gave Detective Lockheart a piece of the sign that Aerie said was left in Sam's kitchen. I figured he would use it to find fingerprints, not to arrest Sam."

"Dan is only doing his job."

"Right. Fine. But Aerie hates me right now and I think she could use your support."

I didn't mention that I was secretly hoping that with Jay there maybe Dan would take it easy on Sam for Aerie's sake. And Aerie would take it easy on me.

Sam was in Detective Lockheart's office. I found Aerie sitting in the reception area. Jay sat next to her and I sat across from him.

"I am really sorry," I said to Aerie.

She took a breath in and looked up at the ceiling, avoiding my gaze.

"I didn't expect Detective Lockheart to use it against him. I thought he could use it to find out who did this."

"He didn't, did he?"

"No," I mumbled.

"I'll talk to Dan. I doubt he plans on arresting him," Jay said.

Aerie dropped her face in her hands. "This is such a mess." She ran her hands up over her hair and tightened her ponytail.

An alarm blurted and then blared. The sound made us all jump in our seats. The bell for the volunteer fire department rang in the next building. Within a minute the engine roared down the street. Jay walked over to the reception desk and asked, "Do you know where they're headed?"

"Spring Creek Plaza. There's a water main break."

We looked at each other. If it was connected and not just a coincidence, this could prove that Sam was innocent of the thefts because obviously somebody else caused the water main break. Or at least we all hoped so. Detective Lockheart came out of his office and threw his arms into the sleeves of his police jacket. He brushed past everyone but pointed a finger at me. "Do not follow me. Do not investigate this. I can handle it." He pushed out the door.

"I doubt it," I said under my breath. I followed him anyway.

Aerie, Jay, and Sam rode together, and I drove myself. There was very little traffic, so we got there right after the fire truck. Grey-brown water gushed out of the theater and poured into the street.

Sam rushed into the pizza shop; Aerie and Jay followed.

Firefighters prepared to pump water and close the leak. Hesitantly, I made my way into The Pizza Pub. Everyone frantically moved boxes off the lower shelves in the kitchen to avoid the slow seep of water onto the floor. I lifted my feet. The water wasn't even half an inch deep but by the looks of the torrent coming out of the theater, that could change any minute.

I ducked into the pizza shop. I had my own kitchen back at the diner and I was very protective of it. I immediately went to work and helped move the boxes and other materials off the floor as quickly as we could.

Suddenly the water rose faster. Soon it was up to my ankles. Sam and Scott ran around the kitchen unplugging anything electrical. There was something very frivolous about trying to save things. There was nothing we could do about the rising water except watch it swallow the entirety of the kitchen floor. I glanced at Sam and saw the hopelessness in his eyes. I wanted to cry for him. We were watching him lose his business.

Outside we could hear the firemen at work. Finally, the water stopped rising. They must have shut off the water. Sam breathed a sigh of relief. Hopefully, he won't lose any of his equipment. Insurance would have to cover the rest. We slogged out of the kitchen. There was nothing more we could do. We stood in the parking lot, which had a slight rise to it and had less water. The theater was even more of a mess.

Firemen pumped water out of the building and down the street. I could hear the water emptying into the storm drains.

The whole scene was disheartening.

Suddenly, a frantic bustle issued from the theater.

Two men slung a third man between them. He was clearly injured and unable to walk on his own. The EMTs raced forward with the gurney and rushed him into the ambulance. I couldn't see who it was, but it didn't look good.

Detective Lockheart stood outside the ambulance talking with one of the EMTs.

As we came closer, I could hear him. "Thank you. I'll call the hospital for an update." He turned around and saw me. He didn't say anything. He just shook his head and walked over to interview one of the firemen.

"I'm going to see what I can find out. Karl is over there." Jay jogged over to where his friend Karl stood. As the general contractor of the site, he might have an idea of what happened. Jay came back a few moments later with the answer. "It looks like someone who knew what they were doing opened the water main."

"Who was injured?" I asked.

"Glen Hensley was electrocuted trying to fix things."

I shivered. "Do they think he will be all right?"

"It doesn't look good. But he was still breathing when they put him in the ambulance."

Sam and Aerie stayed behind. Sam had already called the insurance company and was waiting for a claim adjuster to arrive. I told Jay I could drive him back, but he said he wanted to wait for Chelsea to pick him up. I understood. It was better if I headed out.

Things were getting real. And the harder that Detective Lockheart pushed me to stay away, the more I felt I needed to find out what was going on.

When I got home, I took Ozzy for a walk. I was halfway to the school when my cell phone rang. It was Aerie. "Glen Hensley died on the way to the hospital."

"Whoa. I understand why you are mad at me, Aerie. But I will find out what's going on."

11

Cara had told me that if I chipped my nails anytime during the week, she would fix them up free of charge. I was going to take advantage of that because the drywall hanging had managed to chip two of my nails.

While I was there, I could ask Cara if she had seen anything prior to the water main leak. The spa's windows weren't used as a light source like they were at the pottery shop. The windows were lavishly decorated with valances and a set of blinds. I had my doubts Cara would have been able to notice anything going on over at the work site. But she did have a number of clients throughout the day, and they all talked. Everyone talked to the hairdresser. It was just a matter of figuring out a way to get her to share that information with me.

"Hey, Cara. How are you doing?"

"Don't tell me you chipped a nail?"

"Hanging drywall was a little harder on them than I expected."

"I did promise. Come on over here and let's fix them."

We sat at the nail counter. "This is nice and relaxing music."

I noticed the change to a more ambient spa-like sound than the local radio station that they played earlier when I had my haircut.

"Yeah, it's Ilsa's idea. She's always finding new ways to improve the spa experience."

"It's nice. Kind of soothing."

"Yeah. But I kind of miss gigging out to my favorite song on the radio. "So how did the drywall hanging go?"

"It's done." I didn't realize how happy I would be to say that. Not with everything else that was going on. But I was thrilled that the kitchen was finally finished.

"Now that you have walls, what's your next step? Paint?"

"You know I hadn't even thought about paint. That's a great idea. I'll have to go next door and talk to Bob."

"I always loved painting the walls. It makes any place look brand-new."

The door to the spa opened. I glanced over my shoulder and saw Sam walk in.

Cara smiled. "I'll be with you in just a moment."

"It's okay, Cara, I can help." Ilsa came from the back room and headed to the front desk.

Sam gave me an uncertain glance but then spoke with Ilsa. "I would like to make an appointment for the couples spa for tomorrow."

"Absolutely. Will 7 p.m. work for you?"

"Yes. Thank you. My name is Sam Andrews."

"Let's find something in the schedule. There we are. We'll see you tomorrow at seven with your partner."

"Thank you." Sam hesitated for a moment and then came over to me. He crouched to meet me at eye level. "Hey, Mira. Can you not say anything to Aerie about it? I want it to be a surprise."

"Okay. No problem. I won't mention anything. She's not really talking to me anyway."

"I get that you had to do what you had to do. No hard feelings. I'm sure Aerie will come around."

"Thanks," was all that I could think to say. He smiled briefly and left the salon.

Cara raised an eyebrow but didn't ask any questions. I didn't feel like volunteering any information about the situation either. So, I changed the subject. "Did you hear one of the workers at the theater site was killed?"

"Killed?"

"He was electrocuted. I guess he was trying to fix the water main or something."

"That's crazy. He died?"

"It's pretty sad. The theater hasn't had anything but bad luck. I've been trying to help find out what's going on."

"Do you think someone is responsible for creating the bad luck?"

"I'm almost positive. And I promised Sam and Aerie that I would keep working at it until I figured out what was going on."

"Well, you're pretty good at it, from what I've heard around town."

"Oh really? You've heard about me?"

"Of course. Every woman that comes in here has a story. And every once in a while, you've been mentioned."

I laughed uncomfortably. "I hope in a good light."

"Most of the time." She giggled. "There. How do they look?"

I admired the slick shine of the blue polish. "Brand-new. Thank you." I reached into my wallet to give her some money.

"No, no. I promised you. You don't have to pay me

anything. Besides don't you have to buy some paint for that kitchen of yours?"

"I do."

"Be sure to let me know what color you choose."

"Will do. Thanks again Cara."

"Have fun painting."

I left the salon without gaining too much information. But it was nice to hear from Sam that he didn't hold it against me.

I OPENED the diner early like I always did. And waited for Aerie to arrive from her yoga class. I didn't know what to expect when she got to the diner.

She came in silently and put on her apron.

"Good morning," I said.

Aerie took out her chalkboard and chalk and turned away to the dining room to greet the customers that had come in for breakfast. As they placed their orders, she wrote them up on the big board without comment. She simply added in writing any additional details that I would need.

I stayed in the kitchen. I didn't try to come out and be sociable. It was obvious Aerie wanted her space. I couldn't think of another way to tell her how sorry I was about the situation. She felt betrayed by me and I felt betrayed by Dan. It was a huge mess. A mess that I was determined to fix.

Finally, I couldn't stay quiet. "Aerie," I caught her attention and she half turned. "I'm going to find out who framed Sam. I promise."

Her lips were pinched in a line. She turned back toward the dining room and left.

During a lull between breakfast and lunch, Aerie hung up her apron. "I have an errand to run, I'll be back before eleven."

And she left. Just like that. She was angry with me and I had no idea how to deal with the situation. Mrs. Orsa was the only one sitting in the dining room and she waved me over. "You come here and sit, Mira." She patted the table, and I took the chair next to her. I let out a deep sigh. "Aerie is mad at me."

"Anyone with eyes can see that." Mrs. Orsa laid her weathered hand on top of mine. "What happened?"

I explained the situation to her. She thought about it for a moment.

"When your friends need help and you help in your own way, they will be upset with you for not doing it the way they want. But in the end, they'll come to understand it was because you care about them that you did what you did. She'll see that in time. And this is Aerie we are talking about; she'll see it sooner than most." Mrs. Orsa squeezed my hand.

I sniffled back tears and nodded. "Thanks, Mrs. Orsa."

A few minutes after Mrs. Orsa had left, Aerie returned.

I assumed she had gone out to see Sam. She looked happier, but it didn't appear that she was going to talk to me yet.

"Jay finished hanging the drywall the other day and I was thinking about picking out paint colors. Would you like to come with me?"

She put her apron on and tied it, thinking. "I don't know, Mira. Maybe, not right now."

"Okay. I understand." I went back into the kitchen trying not to feel hurt. But maybe Mrs. Orsa was right. I would have to give her some time.

12

I walked into Bob's Hardware. If I needed to be patient with Aerie, I had to focus on something else, and that would be the new walls in my kitchen.

"Ms. Michaels, it's so nice to see you again."

"Hi, Bob." I took his hand when he offered it. "It's good to see you, too."

"What can I help you with today?"

"I am thinking of painting my kitchen."

"The drywall is finished?" He rubbed his hands together.

"Yep, and I figured I should start painting."

"Right this way." I followed behind Bob to a back wall that held millions of little paint chips in color order. How was I going to pick one from all of this?

Bob must have noticed my expression. "Now, now, don't worry. You'll want to focus on these over here. These are meant for kitchens and bathrooms. You will probably also want to choose a lighter color because it will make the space seem bigger. So that leaves out all of these colors." He waved his hand along the section of paint chips. "So, you see, you really only have to select from this group right here."

I took a deep breath and nodded. "How do I know if it's the right color?"

"You can always take home samples and try them out first. That way you can select the one you like the best."

"Thanks, Bob. I guess I'll be here for a bit." I shifted my weight between my feet and stared at the wall of paint chips.

"Just give me a shout when you need some help."

"Thanks." I stared at the wall for about five minutes, threw caution to the wind grabbed three paint chips in varying shades of yellow and walked over to the counter where Bob was waiting.

"That was fast."

"The sooner I start, the sooner I'll be done." I couldn't make any decisions today. I just wanted to start.

"Okay, give me a few minutes to mix up the sample colors for you. You can find four-inch paintbrushes over there. You'll need one to test these beauties out."

I found the aisle with the paintbrushes and found a cheap four-inch brush that wasn't so cheap and headed back over to the counter.

Bob put the cap on the third jar of paint. "You know I wanted to show you something. I looked into the missing inventory."

"Really?"

"Yep, I also went back in and reviewed some of the security camera footage."

"Oh? Did you find anyone?" Curiosity was getting the better of me.

"I did. I did. And I'd like you to take a look at it for me."

"Have you shown it to Detective Lockheart yet?"

"No. I plan to call him today. But you're the one that asked me, so I figured you would want to know."

"Absolutely. I'd love to see what you found out." I was thrilled to get the scoop before the detective.

"Let me just put the paint in a bag here for you, and let's head to the office. I can bring up the video clips that I saved."

Bob bagged the paint, took the brush from me, put it in the bag, and we walked to his office.

"If you remember, the items that were missing were random. Nothing overly expensive either. Bungee cords, a wrench set, a few carabiners."

We entered his office and Bob pulled a chair next to his desk for me to sit in. I looked around the room. It felt cozier than the polished shine of the store. His office was an organized mess. The two bookshelves were completely packed with books propped on top of other books. A workbench to the left held random tools and some engine or something like that that had been taken apart. Bob's desk had little sticky notes tacked up on every open surface.

"Here we go." Bob turned his monitor in my direction. The video was in black-and-white and from a high angle looking down into the store. He pointed to a man as he entered the lawn mower show area. He was of slender build, had a baseball cap pulled down low, a light jacket, and wearing a pair of jeans and work boots. The work boots didn't mean much. A lot of men around this area wore them. Jay did. Devon did as well. But it could also be one of the workers in the plaza.

We followed him as he walked to the back of the store and disappeared behind an aisle.

"This is where we can look at camera two." He pointed to the video in the corner of the screen. The man slid something into his pocket. "I believe this is where he steals the carabiners."

"Does he steal everything in one visit?"

"No. It was over three different visits. Each time he purchased something small and inexpensive. This time it's a soda from the refrigerator. The next time it's a pack of gum. We keep that stuff at the front counter."

"So, the same guy steals all of the things that are currently missing?"

"Yes. Only I can't make out his face. I'm hoping that Detective Lockheart will have some kind of imaging software, something to figure it out."

"I nodded. "He probably does. Can you let me know if you find out who it is?"

Bob shrugged. "I don't see why not. Detective Lockheart will probably arrest him once we find out who it is. It's less than $500 worth of product. But he's on the video stealing three separate times. He could see jail time, the poor soul."

"I suppose once the theater is finished, he won't be around."

"That's very true. And good riddance then. I hope he learns his lesson."

"Thanks for sharing this with me. I appreciate it. I really want to find out who's behind all of this business framing Sam."

"I would too. It seems very unfair."

We walked outside of his office back to the counter. "Thanks for the paint. How much do I owe you?" I asked.

"Not a thing. It's a gift to get you started." Bob smiled like Santa Claus.

"Are you sure? I mean, you just had stuff stolen."

"It wasn't by you. I want to make sure you get started on

your kitchen. You let me know which color you like the best."

I was really grateful to Bob. "I can do that." Every little bit of money that I saved could go back into the appliances. "Thanks again, Bob. I'll talk to you later."

"Have a nice afternoon, Ms. Michaels."

THE LIGHTING in the kitchen wasn't very good. I supposed I would have to wait until tomorrow to see the effect of the sunlight would have on the three boxes that I had painted on the wall with the different shades of yellow paint.

I would've brought Arnold in here to help me decide on color choices except that the last time he and I painted together he ended up looking more like a skunk from rubbing his tail up against my paint spattered pant leg. Once this was dry, I would bring him in here to get his honest opinion. In the glow of the kitchen light, I couldn't really tell the difference between them. I stepped back to take a better look when I heard the faint sound of knocking at my front door. Maybe Jay was coming by to pick up some of his equipment that he had left here.

I stepped through the open door frame; the back door was still on backorder. I walked around to the front of the house. I could see the back of Detective Lockheart, his jacket without a single wrinkle, as he knocked on my door. For a split second, I considered sneaking back the way I had come. But he heard me and turned.

"Oh, there you are."

"Why are you here?" My hands were already on my hips.

He stuffed his hands in the pockets of the windbreaker he was wearing. The evening had turned cool, and goosebumps rose on my arms. When he didn't immediately respond, I turned, and he followed me into the backyard toward the kitchen.

"I came because I wanted to apologize." He actually sounded sincere.

I swung around with the paintbrush in hand, but detective Lockheart had been closer than I thought and got a chest full of paint. "Oh, my goodness. I'm so sorry." And the fact I was apologizing made me mad.

"Well, this brightens up my windbreaker." He laughed. "It's okay." He paused. "I do owe you an apology." A roll of paper towels sat on the stool in the kitchen. He reached past me and tore off a few sheets.

"You owe me a lot of apologies I've never gotten."

"Maybe that's true. But I know the current situation you're in is a little different than before."

"What you mean?"

"Jay told me I may have created a bit of a rift between you and Aerie."

"Where does he get off telling you what's going on between me and Aerie?"

"Don't get mad at Jay. He saw how miserable the two of you are and pointed out to me that I might have been able to handle the situation a bit differently. And he's right." He rubbed the towels on his jacket. The paint spread.

I grabbed a couple of paper towels and wiped the remaining paint off of the brush. The brush would have to be washed before the paint dried, so I was determined this conversation would end quickly.

"You said you were sorry. Actually, now that I think about it, no you haven't."

"I apologize. Really, I do."

"Thank you, and now leave." I actually made a shooing

motion with my hands but that only seemed to amuse him. "Look, I have a lot to do tonight."

"I see." He surveyed the new walls. "Is this the paint you got from Bob today?"

"How would you know?"

"He called and talked to me about the video surveillance that he had regarding some petty theft from his store last week."

Dan had talked to Bob about me.

"So, I bought some paint." Which was kind of a lie because Bob didn't charge me anything.

"Bob told me that he showed you the video."

"Okay, so what?" Was he going to yell at me about that too?

"Do you know who it is?" he asked.

"It's not Sam." I told him.

"No. It's not. It's Milo Archer."

"One of Karl's guys."

"Yes. I figured you would want to know. But I also wanted to ask you if you had any additional information that might help."

"I thought you didn't want me interfering."

"I don't, but I will admit you look at things different than I do and that occasionally gets results."

"Occasionally? You're really selling this, that you appreciate the work that I do."

"Sorry. Look. If you know anything about Milo and if there's any way his shoplifting could be linked to the stealing of the sign, I can stop pressuring Sam." He shifted his weight. "And I think it's what both of us want."

I stood there for a moment. "I can't think of any reason for Milo to plant a piece of the theater sign in Sam's kitchen. I can't see why Milo would frame Sam. That wouldn't make any sense. All I know is Milo is short on cash."

Detective Lockheart's eyes lit up at the mention of that. "Really?"

I continued. "Yeah, one of the guys said Milo's been hard up for a while and this is his first job in a long time. So yeah, it makes sense he would shoplift."

Detective Lockheart paced. "If Milo was low on funds, that would be motive for stealing the crane. I know he frequented Sam's restaurant, which could explain the flour." He strode back and forth again. "The theft from Bob's hardware is minor. But theft of the crane is a felony. I would just have to find a way to prove it." He mumbled this last bit. But then he suddenly looked up at me. "This does not mean that you should try to help me prove this. I can do that on my own."

First, he wants my help, then he doesn't want my help. "Good luck then."

"Continue with your kitchen painting. Don't worry about this." He turned to go.

"You realize you're the most condescending person I've ever met?"

"What?"

He seriously didn't understand.

"I would try to explain it to you but that might be too much. Good night, Detective Lockheart."

He turned to go and then spun back. "I don't mean to be condescending."

"Okay then."

"I am sorry for the predicament I put you in with Aerie." He stepped closer.

"Yes, yes. You said you were sorry. Thank you very much. Good night."

"Good night, Ms. Michaels."

He walked out the open space, still in need of a door. I let out the breath I was holding. But two seconds later Detective Lockheart reappeared.

"You do have this room secured from the rest of the house, correct?"

I pointed to the plywood board nailed across the dining room entrance. "Yes."

"Good. Have a good night." He turned and left. I stood there for a moment wondering what had just happened.

13

I had a hard time falling asleep. I tossed and turned for a while. Dan Lockheart did that to me, confused me, irritated me and kept my mind racing. First, he yelled at me, then he made me mad, and after all of that, he apologized to me. After I fell asleep, the next thing I remember was Arnold walking back and forth across my head on the pillow. "Shoo, I'm trying to sleep," I mumbled. His whiskers tickled my eyes. I blinked them open to find him staring me in the face.

Wake up.

"Wha?" I sat up groggily. In the hallway, Ozzy yipped twice. "What is going on, you guys? I want to sleep."

The bed was warm and cozy, pillows were nice and fluffy, I wanted to go back to sleep. As I laid my head back on the pillow, a scraping-scratching kind of sound came from downstairs. Ozzy yipped again, this time louder.

"Crap." I grabbed the flashlight next to my bed. I was awake now, adrenaline zinging in all my muscles. It worked better than any caffeine, that's for sure. I took a deep breath. Probably a squirrel or something. Either way, I had to take care of it or the animals wouldn't sleep, and therefore I wouldn't sleep.

I made my way downstairs, ears tuned to the slightest sounds. Nothing. I walked down the hallway flipping on all the lights as I went past the living room and into the dining room. I peeked out the front window. Nobody was at the door. And then I heard it. A faint shuffling from the other side of the plywood between me and the kitchen.

It had to be the squirrels again. The broom was still in the kitchen from cleaning up the drywall dust.

I didn't want them building nests in there, so, with my flashlight in one hand and plans of shooing them out with the broom, I marched out the front door barefoot and in my pajamas.

Halfway through the side yard, I stepped on a stone and realized I should have put on those flip-flops next to the front door. *Squirrels*. They are going to see the underside of that broom when I get in there.

I marched through the backyard. Wait. Something was different. I backtracked two steps. The stepstool had been moved. Earlier it had been near the door. Now it was under the window. Squirrels can't move something that heavy. I swung the flashlight up. My heart skipped a beat. A dark human form was moving around in the kitchen.

A curse slipped out of my mouth before I realized making any noise was a bad idea.

It didn't matter. The intruder had been alerted by my flashlight beam. He charged me like a raging bull. Before I could even raise the flashlight to swing it, the black form slammed me to the ground, the wind knocked out of me, I felt like a fish on land. For a moment, everything went black. I saw stars and nothing else. By the time I could force air back into my lungs, the prowler was gone.

I listened hard but couldn't hear any footsteps. I crawled up off the ground and limped my way to the front door, which stood wide open. For a moment I was worried the intruder might have entered the house. But both Arnold and Ozzy were waiting for me inside the door. I still couldn't stand up straight. Between my bruised ribs and my aching head I wanted to curl into a ball. But I made my way upstairs to my cell phone and called 911.

I closed and locked my front door, grabbed a can of soda to soothe my sore throat and steady my breathing, and waited until someone arrived. I really hoped it wouldn't be Dan Lockheart.

TO MY RELIEF it wasn't. Tyler Stewart knocked on my front door about ten minutes later.

Tyler was twenty-something, with broad shoulders and an awkward eagerness to help. He listened to me tell him everything that happened. "Can you think of any other details about this person? How tall they were? If they were skinny or heavyset?"

I shook my head; the movement made me nauseous. Concussion? It would serve me right for assuming it was squirrels.

"Whoever it was charged me when I shined the flashlight in their direction. It was seconds between when I saw them and when I was on my back with the wind knocked out of me. They weren't exceptionally tall, I guess, but they were hunched over to take me out. I couldn't really tell anything about their features."

He wrote quickly. "Can you walk me through where everything happened?"

"Sure." This time I put on the flip-flops.

"I heard a shuffling noise in the kitchen, and I thought it was squirrels. I had the flashlight with me and went outside." I held up the Maglite and Officer Stewart followed me out the front door. We walked around the side of the house and into the backyard.

"This is where I was standing when I raised the flashlight and saw someone in the kitchen. The light spooked them, and they ran out and tackled me. And I fell here." I pointed to the mashed grass. I stood still and looked back at the kitchen trying to envision the intruder to see if I could jog my memory for any new details. Something caught my eye in the kitchen. I took a few steps closer and realized what it was. I couldn't breathe. It was as if I got hit all over again. Every brand-new wall of the kitchen was covered in dripping blue-black graffiti.

By the time officer Stewart left it was close to 5 a.m. I couldn't go back to sleep. I made myself some semblance of breakfast: strawberry iced pop tarts and a large cup of tea. I would cook myself something more substantial later at the diner. I was so disheartened. It felt as if I would never cook in my own home. The odds were obviously against it ever happening.

A whine from Ozzy woke me out of the downward spiral when I realized she needed to go for a walk.

"Okay, girl, let's go." I got her leash and clipped it on to her collar. "You did a good job last night waking me up." I patted her fuzzy head.

What about me? Arnold scorned.

"You were fabulous. Without you waking me, I could have avoided getting the wind knocked out of me."

If you didn't sleep like the dead, it would be easier. Maybe next time I should try biting you?

"No. No, let's not go there." I gave Arnold a pat on the head and a treat, and headed outside with Ozzy.

The sun was coming up, bathing everything in a bright orange-pink glow. It would have been beautiful if I weren't so despondent about the damage done to the kitchen. All of Jay's hard work and I wasn't sure how we would be able to paint over the graffiti.

Ozzy stopped to pee on a bush. A car came toward me. Dan Lockheart was behind the wheel. I turned my head away and looked up into the morning sky, hoping against all hope he was driving to some other person's house. But no such luck. He parked behind my beat-up Buick.

I supposed I had best face this head-on. I turned around with Ozzy and headed back to the house. Detective Lockheart got out of his car as I came closer. "It's good to see you're not damaged after last night's episode," he said.

"I'm more irritated than damaged. That jerk graffitied my brand-new kitchen."

"No forced entry?"

"You read the report." I knew he had, or he wouldn't be here.

"Did you get a good look at the intruder?" His notepad was already in hand.

"No. I told Officer Stewart that I did not. They bum-rushed me and before I knew it, I was flat on my back seeing stars and sucking wind."

He looked up from taking notes. "Did you get checked for a concussion?"

"I don't have a concussion."

"If you saw stars, it's very possible you could have a concussion. You should have had the EMTs check you out." Now he was glaring at me.

I looked at him sideways. "What's with the heightened concern for my well-being?"

"Officer Stewart should have called the EMTs to have you checked out. He didn't, and I will be putting that in his report."

"You're an awfully strict boss," I mused.

"There are guidelines to go by, and when they're followed the job is properly completed. And when they're not, it's sloppy. I won't have sloppy in my police station."

"I see. Is there anything else you need?" I was impatient to get on with my day.

"Can you walk me through what happened last night?" The pen scratched across the notebook.

"I took Officer Stewart through all of this. And I need to open the diner soon." From where I stood in my front yard I could see the diner with its kitchen that beckoned me, where I planned to hide for the rest of the day.

"Mrs. Orsa will understand if her muffin is a few minutes late this morning."

I gave him a hard look. Who was he to tell me when I could open the diner? "You're not leaving until I tell you everything, are you?"

"No."

I shook my head. I walked him through everything step-by-step.

"And you didn't get a look at his or her face?"

"No. They had something like a hat or mask on." My annoyance seeped through the words.

"So, give me your best hunch. Who do you think it was? Male or female?"

"I don't know." Detective Lockheart was so frustrating. How was I supposed to guess who hit me? I had been flat on my back, sucking air for most of the experience.

"Why don't you find evidence? That idiot ruined my kitchen."

"As if on cue, Jay walked across the street from the house he shared with Aerie.

"What's this about the kitchen? Are you okay?" Jay shook Dan's hand while looking me over.

"I'm fine." I turned to Detective Lockheart. "You should take notes. That's a nice way to check on someone. First, ask if they're okay."

"I did ask you if you were okay. You should have been checked out by the EMTs and I'll have a word with Officer Stewart about that."

"Don't get all up in Officer Stewart's face about this. I'm fine."

Jay waited for us to finish arguing and then asked, "Can I see the kitchen?"

"Of course. But I don't think you're going to like what you see." We walked to the backyard and when Jay saw the damage, he let fly a couple expletives. "Sorry. Black paint is impossible to paint over. I might as well hang new drywall."

"Really?" I cringed. "I can't afford new drywall."

Jay saw my anxiety. "Don't worry about it, Mira, I'll figure out some way to pay for it."

The detective turned to me. "Have you thought of a security system?"

"Detective Lockheart, I just said I can't pay for decent drywall. Do you really think I can afford to install a security system?"

"Obviously, someone is aware that you are looking into the current situation over at the theater and they are trying to dissuade you. And if—"

"If you think this will stop me from trying to find out what's going on, you have got to be kidding me. If anything,

I'm more determined to find the jerk that did this and make them pay." I took Ozzy by the leash and left the men to the backyard. "I need to open the diner." I didn't want to talk about drywall or the theater or anything else today. I just wanted to lose myself in cooking. And maybe the kind, smiling face of Mrs. Orsa who was probably waiting for her muffin.

14

As expected, by the time I got to the diner a line had formed. Mrs. Orsa was patiently waiting along with a few of the workers from the theater work site.

"Sorry, Mrs. Orsa, for being late this morning, I had some issues at my house."

"Oh, I see Detective Lockheart is there. Is he your new sweetheart?"

I almost choked. "Of course not. He's at my house because last night someone spray-painted graffiti in my new kitchen. Detective Lockheart is collecting evidence."

"Someone vandalized your new kitchen? That's awful."

I nodded. It was awful. And I would find out who did this. "Jay put in a lot of hard work in the kitchen. He said he might have to do it again. I just don't know if I have the cash to pay for more drywall."

Mrs. Orsa patted my arm. "Don't you worry about that, honey, things will work out." I smiled a tiny smile. Mrs. Orsa always looked at the bright side of everything.

I headed back into the kitchen to start up the grill. Aerie arrived shortly afterward and, without a sound, turned on the coffee maker and got Mrs. Orsa her muffin. I expected another day of angry silence from Aerie until she stopped me in the kitchen and gave me a huge hug. "I saw Jay and Dan combing through your backyard. What happened?"

"Some jerk graffitied my kitchen."

"Jay told me he'll have to hang new drywall."

"Aerie, I don't know what I'm going to do." A feeling of panic swept over me, but I pushed it away and took a deep breath, "I don't want to think about it right now. I can always cook at the diner."

"Of course, you can. Whenever you want." Aerie put on her apron and grabbed her small board and chalk. The diner was filling up and she had to take orders. I needed to start grilling the breakfast basics.

The good thing about being a short-order cook was that once I got going, I couldn't think about anything except filling orders. I took the bacon and eggs from the refrigerator and the ingredients to start a fresh batch of pancake batter.

I worked quickly, cooking the meals that Aerie had transferred to the large chalkboard, plating and lining them on the counter for her to take to the tables. I focused on work and it kept my brain busy. I didn't let my mind wander onto the house and the work that had to be done there. After the first few hours it slowed down a bit. I craved some ice cream, so I walked out to the front.

We had sold quite a bit of the creamy goodness over the last week, which was good to see. I scraped the last of the chocolate raspberry and put it in a dish. I leaned my back against the wall and people-watched everyone eating their breakfast. Aerie was chatting away at a table on the right with Cara and Ilsa.

I glanced at my nails. The bright teal reminded me that a

beach vacation was now only going to exist in my imagination. My manicure was holding up well, which said something.

I scanned the room. Mrs. Orsa had already left. The workers hadn't though, which surprised me. A couple of them were ogling Cara and Ilsa. I guessed work hadn't started back up at the worksite yet.

Aerie came back to put another order on the board. "Cara is celebrating five years at the spa today. Ilsa is treating her to breakfast."

"I'll have to congratulate her. And thank her. My manicure held up after all of the drama and trauma of the night."

"It'll be okay, Mira, I promise." She gave me a hug. The diner cleared quickly after that. Everyone had places to go. And I couldn't keep thoughts of my ruined kitchen out of my head any longer.

"Someone was trying to intimidate me to stop investigating the worksite. That's not going to happen. I'm more determined now than ever to figure this out."

"I'd like to help you if you'll let me." Aerie gave me another huge hug.

"Of course."

DETECTIVE LOCKHEART CAME in for a late lunch around two. The diner had cleared out by then and it was just Aerie and me. I grilled up his daily lunch of hamburger and french fries. Aerie was still angry with the detective about the accusations against Sam, and she refused to talk to him, so she spent her time at the farthest point from the counter wiping down the tables.

I handed Detective Lockheart his plate of hamburger and fries. "You know you should try Aerie's vegan burgers every once in a while."

He ignored the suggestion. "I have some evidence from your house."

I didn't want to think about it, but the curiosity got the better of me. "What did you find?"

"We picked up an imprint of the shoe the perp wore last night."

"What do you do with that? Stare at everybody's shoes in town?"

"No, but it's evidence." He leaned very close. "I would stay away from Sam Andrews for the moment. I would advise Aerie to do the same."

"Why?" I practically shouted it and Aerie turned her head in our direction.

"Because I think it might be him, I think Glen's electrocution was an accident."

"Did Jay put you up to this because he doesn't like Sam and he doesn't want his sister dating him?"

"No, not at all." He shook his head.

"You're going to assume that it was Sam that did this to my home?"

"Look, I don't want to argue with you today. I know you've been through a lot. I'm just giving you my professional advice."

"I think you need to get your head out of your butt. It wasn't Sam." But even as I said those words, I flashed back to the moment I was hit and thrown to the ground. No. It couldn't have been Sam. Could it? "It wasn't him."

Detective Lockheart searched my eyes, a warm shiver went down my spine. "Okay. I won't mention it again. Thank you for lunch." He put a twenty-dollar bill on the counter and got up to leave. He always paid too much for lunch.

"Aerie..."

She came over from wiping down the same table fifteen times while I was talking with Detective Lockheart.

"What happened between Dan, Sam, and your brother?"

"It's silly, really."

"Obviously not to Dan and Jay."

"Well, back in high school, the three of them were friends. Actually, they were more like the Three Musketeers. You never saw one without the others." She slowly folded the cleaning rag that smelled of lemon oil. "The three of them were always doing things together. They even built the shed back behind our house. It was a Father's Day gift for my dad. Dan and Sam loved my dad just as much as we did." She grinned and I could tell she was seeing it all as she remembered. "I think it was mostly because he fed the boys whenever they came into the diner.

"Then our parents passed away and things got really hard for Jay. He was eighteen and graduating from high school. But he had to go to court to gain guardianship over me or I would end up in foster care. It was pretty traumatic, but we managed to make it through that okay. Dan was very supportive. But for some reason Sam kind of lost his way. I hadn't realized it at the time, but I think my dad took the place of Sam's own dad. So, when Dad died Sam took it hard. Harder than you would think. That began the crazy days for Sam. He didn't have anyone else. Anyway, one day he stole a car to take for a joyride. He put it back where he found it but when he was asked about the situation, he pointed the finger at Dan."

I nodded my head. Now I understood.

"I'm guessing Dan's always been on the straight and narrow?"

"He was thoroughly insulted that anyone would even think that he would steal a car. But worst of all, he felt betrayed by Sam. Jay had a real problem with it too. He felt like Sam turned his back on both of them. But I know Sam was hurting and that's what caused all of the problems."

"Now I get it. Dan got his panties all in a bunch over Sam telling everyone it had been him. And Jay is just loyal as crap."

"That's pretty much it."

"I don't know who destroyed my kitchen and knocked me down yesterday. But it wasn't Sam."

Aerie came around the counter and gave me a hug again.

"We'll figure this out," I told her.

"Do you have a plan?"

15

"Yes. I want to talk to Heather at Pocket Moon Pottery. Will you come with me?" I told Aerie.

"Why talk to her?" she asked.

"She has this great window that looks out onto the parking lot in front of the theater."

"Okay. I'll drive."

Once we got in the car, I could tell Aerie was waiting to ask me something.

"What did Dan say about Sam?" Aerie needed to know.

"He still thinks it's him; he thinks the electrocution was an accident."

"What do you think?"

"I think someone is framing Sam, and that Detective Lockheart is letting his past with Sam cloud his ability to solve this case."

"So, it's our job to help." Aerie stated it like truth.

"Absolutely. Game?"

"Of course, I'm game." She settled into the driver's seat.

The dashboard clock said it was two-thirty p.m. "If we

want to talk to Heather, we need to get there soon. The three o'clock birthday parties can be pretty insane."

"The parties can get insane?" She grinned that mischievous grin of hers.

"Don't get any ideas." Had I even told Aerie when my birthday was?

Aerie kept her eyes on the road, but she continued to smile.

"I'm serious. No one wants a birthday party. Namely me."

"What if I want to have one?"

"Then I'll have a birthday party at Pocket Moon for you. And I'll invite all your friends."

"Can you imagine Dan, Jay, and Sam all in one room together?"

"Actually, that's even more incentive. Consider it done." I cackled with laughter.

"I'm beginning to believe that you enjoy stirring up trouble."

"You're just realizing that now?" I chided.

"I think that's why I like you." She took a deep breath and gripped the steering wheel.

"Well, that's good because I don't think it will change anytime soon."

Aerie pulled into the parking lot and parked in front of Pocket Moon Pottery. We watched a line of five-year-olds making their way into the shop.

"Oh boy. This one could be a doozy today."

"They are so cute," Aerie cooed.

"Yeah? Kind of like puppies. Let's see if we can catch Heather before she gets too busy."

"I suddenly want to paint something." Aerie wriggled her fingers.

"Your boyfriend is being framed, remember? We're here to get information."

"Yes, yes. Okay, fine." She pouted.

We followed a mom who was busy herding cats, getting all the five-year-olds back into the party room without picking up and/or breaking anything in the shop.

Heather expertly assisted the mom by directing the kids away from the shelves. She waved when she saw me. "I need to talk to you. But let me get this settled down first."

I nodded to her. "We'll just look around."

Aerie immediately went to a shelf full of garden figures. "Oh, I want to paint a gnome." She picked one up. "How about this little guy?"

I rolled my eyes. "You're serious, aren't you?"

"If we have to wait..."

"Go for it. I'll help you pick out the paint colors."

Aerie sat down at one of the empty tables with her stack of paints and picked up the small sponge that lay on the table. With it she wiped the clay dust from the little figure. That's when the train of five-year-olds exited the birthday room, and were instructed to choose a piece of pottery to paint for the party.

Kids were told to choose from one shelf. The figurines. Easy enough. Unicorns and swords were the big winners. Everything was pretty copacetic until the birthday girl noticed the fairy house on the other side of the room. "I want that one." She pointed frantically. After a bit of coaxing from the parent and stoic determination on the side of the child, tears ensued. From both of them.

Heather masterfully guided the child back to the original shelf of figurines and explained the importance of joining her friends in completing one of these figures. The birthday girl settled on one of the unicorns when Heather mentioned that she could put glitter on hers after it was painted.

Once each child was settled with their figurines and pots of paint, Heather came out of the back room to sit with us. "How are you ladies doing?"

"We're doing well. But we're still working on the problems over at the theater."

"I did want to talk to you about that."

"Have you seen something?"

Aerie abandoned her gnome.

"I think so. I noticed the big guy having an argument with the guy that always wears a baseball cap pulled down over his eyes."

"The big guy is Travis." I knew his weight well. Unfortunately.

"The baseball cap guy might be Ron or Milo," said Aerie.

"They were arguing in the parking lot. There was a lot of screaming. They threatened each other back and forth for a while before the head guy broke it up and told them both to go back to work. But I noticed neither of them worked near each other for the rest of the day."

It wasn't surprising to hear that Travis was fighting with someone. But it wasn't necessarily helpful.

"Anything else happen lately?" I asked.

"The insurance adjusters came. And Noah Weller was there to speak with them. He didn't look too happy."

I nodded. "The damage to the theater was extensive."

"The opening is obviously going to be delayed, I'd imagine."

Heather tapped her watch. "Let me check on how the party is going. I'll be right back. There might be something else you should hear."

She disappeared into the back room. Aerie was happily

painting her gnome when police sirens blared. All four police cars pulled into the parking lot in front of the theater. The next events played out like a movie through the shop's front window.

"Now what's going on?" I walked to the entrance.

"Something big." Aerie and I stepped outside the store to get a closer look. Once there, we heard someone mention a body. Aerie's hand flew to her mouth. "Oh, goodness."

Scott from The Pizza Pub stood on the sidewalk watching the scene. Aerie and I walked in the direction of the theater.

We weren't the only ones mindlessly drawn to the scene at the theater. Cara and Ilsa joined us.

"Did someone just say they found a body?" Cara asked.

"I think that's what I heard." We stared at the theater. Cara jostled Aerie and Ilsa bumped into me as we watched. I recognized her perfume.

THE POLICE ASKED everyone to go back inside. Cara and Ilsa walked back into the spa. Aerie and I continued across the parking lot to Detective Lockheart, who was getting out of his car. Officer Stewart was already standing at the front of the theater.

Dan shouted to the officer. "I want you to arrest Milo Archer. I'm going to see about this body."

"Yes, sir." Officer Stewart saw me and raised a tentative hand to wave, then turned to enter the theater.

"I think someone has a crush on you," Aerie whispered to me.

"Stop. After the graffiti incident, he just helped nurse the bump on my head."

"I bet he did." Aerie snickered.

"Okay. Enough. Let's go see what's going on."

Detective Lockheart disappeared into the trees behind the theater.

When the officers were preoccupied, I grabbed Aerie's wrist and tugged her over to the other side of the building. "Come on, we can get into the woods this way."

"You really want to see a body?" she asked tentatively even though she kept in step with me.

"I want to find out who it is."

"I don't know." Aerie tugged away in an effort to go back to the parking lot.

"You don't have to come with me."

"Fine. But you know Dan is going to have a fit if he sees you there."

"Maybe. I'll stay hidden."

Aerie gave me a look. "That's highly improbable."

She was right. I somehow had a problem with staying silent and hidden when it was important to do so. Sprained ankles and spilled paint came to mind.

Aerie followed me as we crunched our way through the underbrush. It would be impossible to sneak up on Detective Lockheart. So instead of us finding him, he found us. I looked up and there he was. "Stop right there. The two of you need to go back to the parking lot."

"Who was killed?" I whisper-shouted.

"We don't know if it was an accidental death or if they were killed. But it appears to be Ron Cain, one of the workers for the theater."

"Really?"

"Do not share that information with anyone. Do either of you know Ron?"

Aerie and I simultaneously replied, "No."

"In any of your..." Detective Lockheart appeared to be thinking of the right word, "...investigations, did you come across anything about him?"

"Actually," I said, "yesterday, Heather from Pocket Moon Pottery saw him or Milo fighting with Travis."

That reminded me that Heather had said she wanted to tell me something before we left. Although, I wouldn't mention it to Detective Lockheart just yet.

The detective pulled out a tiny notebook and took notes. "You two can follow behind me but stay back. I can't have you disrupting the area any more than you already have."

I gave him a dark look. I wanted to yell at him and defend myself, but I knew better at this point. He was letting us see the scene of the crime. Which is more than he usually would. Which probably meant he was desperate for information.

Aerie and I stayed about fifteen feet away from the body. Personally, I didn't want to get any closer.

"It looks like blunt force trauma to the head," Dan said without taking his eyes off the body.

"Like a stone or something?" The forest floor was littered with dead leaves and pine needles. But every few feet, a rock poked out from beneath the decay.

"It appears he may have been dragged. Officer Jones can you follow me and take photos?"

Detective Lockheart and the woman from the reception area at the police station, now holding a camera, walked in the direction the victim's feet were pointing.

I could see the path where his feet had been dragged. The leaves parted to make zigzags in the soil.

"So, this means he was killed somewhere else. Right?" I asked Detective Lockheart.

"Yes. But where?"

Aerie and I followed them at a distance.

"Whoever dragged him out here hid the initial point of entry into the woods." Detective Lockheart wrote additional information in his little book.

"I need to get more officers into the woods to search. There could be evidence in the underbrush."

"Yes sir," Officer Jones responded. She had finished taking photos and marched her way toward the parking lot.

Detective Lockheart wiped his forehead. "Anyone could have driven the body here and parked in the lot and pulled him into the woods to dump the body here." He slipped the notebook back into his pocket. "I'd appreciate it if you guys kept the information to yourselves. But if you hear anything, please let me know."

Before we left, I asked about the one thing that had been on my mind since Detective Lockheart arrived. "Why are you arresting Milo Archer, do you think he did it?"

"No. We found out he has ties with smugglers who sold the crane in Harrisburg. But I will probably question him about the murder as well. I can't make any assumptions that Milo killed Ron."

"Right. Assumptions don't lead to good detective work," I said.

Detective Lockheart gave me a look. I was actually being serious, but it appeared that he thought I was joking around.

"Aerie and I will let you know if we hear anything." I walked up the slope, crunching through the underbrush, toward the parking lot, watching the ground for clues. Aerie followed.

Once we got to the parking lot, Aerie knew something was up. "What are you thinking?"

"I'm thinking we need to talk to Karl."

"Why?"

"Someone killed Ron. Who would want to kill Ron? I could name a couple people."

"I don't think you'll have the opportunity right now. Detective Lockheart is going to talk to him first."

"Let's see if Jay can help us out with that."

Aerie pulled out her phone and dialed Jay's number. She explained the situation and hung up. "He said he'll help. He'll be able to talk to Karl this evening. He doesn't recommend that we come with him, though. He'll call if Karl is willing to talk to us in person."

"I figured as much. Karl might be more willing to share information if Jay is alone. But it would be much better if we could ask questions directly."

16

The call came about two hours later. Karl was willing to meet with me, but only me, and only as long as Jay was there.

"Sorry, Aerie."

"It's fine, really. I want to find out who has done this and is framing Sam. If I can't talk to them, I'm glad it's you. Just find out what is going on."

Jay wanted me to meet him at The Pizza Pub. Jay and Karl were sitting in a booth near the door. I could see Sam in the back, and I could tell that he was curious, but he didn't come over.

"Hey, Mira. Can you tell Karl what you know?"

"I was hoping that Karl could tell me what he knows." I slid into the booth next to Jay.

"You've been looking into this for a while. Karl's been trying to cope with keeping things together at the worksite. Maybe, if you tell him what you found out so far, he might be able to add some pieces."

"Okay, well, I know from Bob that someone had been stealing from his store. The police believe it was Milo pilfering items to help him steal the crane. There was also the fight during karaoke." I shifted in my seat as I remembered Travis falling on me. "Then there was Ron's body behind the theater. Dan isn't pointing fingers because the body could have been brought in by anyone pulling into the parking lot. Although I think he still has eyes on Sam."

"Ron had a fight with Travis yesterday that I had to break up. You ever hear anything around what they fought about the other night?"

"All I remember is Ron called Travis a drunk or lush or something."

"Did anybody find out anything about the theater sign, or who opened the water main?"

Karl straightened. "The water pipe had to have been opened by one of my guys. I told Detective Lockheart that. The only person that would know how to open one of those up and have the tools would be somebody from my crew."

"What about Noah Weller? What do you know about him?"

"He is a nervous wreck is what he is. I'm pretty sure he'll go bankrupt at this point. Even if the theater manages to open sometime in the future."

"Do you think he could have done this: kill Ron? If so, why Ron?"

Both Jay and Karl snorted. "Ron was a class one jerk. Even I wanted to kill him." He shifted in his seat. "I guess I shouldn't say that."

"Not until they find the killer," I said. "Dan likes to arrest people willy-nilly."

"No, he doesn't," Jay defended. "He's just doing his job."

I gave Jay the side eye. "I have a gut feeling that it's none of your guys. But I really don't know who it could be if it's not Noah Weller."

"I suppose it could be Weller but why would he kill Ron?"

"He would kill Ron if Ron was the one that opened up the pipe."

"Of course. That water main leak caused a ton of damage. It pretty much ensured that Noah Weller would go bankrupt."

"Why would Ron want Noah to go bankrupt?"

"Besides being a huge jerk, Ron liked to threaten people. It wouldn't surprise me if Ron had threatened Noah to see if he could squeeze more money out of him."

"Noah wouldn't pay so then Ron opens the water main?"

"That could happen."

"I have a friend at the bank who might be able to help us take a look at some bank statements." I shifted my glance to Jay. "Don't tell Dan, okay?"

"Yeah, no worries." He waved it off.

I continued, "Weller and Cain are not local residents, but I'll see if she can help."

"Thanks Mira, that would be really great. I'd like to get the heat off of me and my crew."

THE NEXT DAY when I walked into the bank's foyer Ellie perked up. "I was wondering when I would see you. I heard about all of the stuff going on at the theater. Did you know that they had already filled the giant fish tank at the movie theater and that two giant goldfish actually survived the electrocution flood? Do you have any good intel to share?"

"I'm here to see if you have anything you can share."

"Mr. Meyer isn't here, so..." Her eyes lit up. "What do you need?"

"I'm wondering if the owner of the theater, Mr. Noah Weller, has paid out any large sums of money lately. Or if Ron Cain has received any large sums of money in his bank account."

Ellie rubbed her hands together. "This sounds juicy."

"We have reason to believe that Noah Weller is going bankrupt. And that Ron Cain may have blackmailed him."

"Who's this Ron Cain guy?"

"He was one of the workers over at the theater. But he was found dead yesterday afternoon."

"Another body? I was thinking about moving to the city, but this place just keeps getting more interesting." Her eyes gleamed. "Neither of these guys is local. I'll have to see if I can hack into some databases."

"Ellie, I don't know if I want you to hack into anything. You could get into trouble."

"Mira, this place bores me," she drawled. "Hacking is fun and exciting, and the threat of exposure is exhilarating. Besides, I have this new boyfriend I met online. And he has skillz with a capital Z."

"If you do this, just swear to me you won't get caught."

"Done. Thanks for bringing me something juicy. I'll call you later."

I left Ellie feeling very guilty. If she got caught, it was on my head. I didn't need any more guilt or more people angry with me. It was too stressful.

17

At the diner, Aerie wrote the next order on the chalkboard. "I'm totally creeped out that Ron's body might have been near us when Sam and I were in the back of the building near those woods for the couple's massage the other evening.

"Oh?"

"Yeah, the spa has a patio in the back with a fireplace roaring. After the massages we sat out there with wine. It was really romantic. Less romantic if it was dead-body-adjacent." She scrunched her nose.

My cell phone rang. It was Ellie. "That was fast."

"I told you my man has skillz."

"Did you find out anything?"

"Of course."

"Spill it."

"You are right about Ron. It looks like he's been getting a thousand dollars every couple of months. But we can't seem to trace it back to anyone, so he must be getting cash."

"Okay, so he was bribing someone?"

"It's a possibility. But get this: Weller doesn't have any

money. Everything that is in his business account is linked back to the theater, or insurance companies or construction companies. His personal account isn't much better. I'm surprised the guy has money to eat lunch."

"So, it doesn't look like the money was coming from Weller?"

"Doubt it. Is there someone else you'd like us to look up?"

"You do realize what you're doing can get you stuck in a federal prison, right?"

"Only if I get caught." Ellie had a bit of a darker side than I had realized.

"I don't think your new boyfriend is a good influence on you, Ellie."

"Maybe not. But it sure is exciting."

"Be careful."

"Always. Let me know if you need anything else, okay?"

"I think I'm good. Thanks, Ellie. Your next breakfast sandwich is on me."

I WASN'T any closer to figuring out who killed Ron. Everyone still suspected Sam, which just didn't make sense to me. Usually when I was working on these mysteries things would suddenly click in my mind. But nothing like that was happening. I didn't know where to look next.

The morning rush was over and everyone but Mrs. Orsa had bought take-out. My breakfast sandwiches were a hit. The kitchen was quiet so I joined Aerie out front. After helping to reset one of the tables, I noticed Mrs. Orsa was still here.

"Hey, Mrs. Orsa." I plopped down in the seat across from her.

"What's wrong, honey? Are you and Aerie still fighting?"

"No. We're fine now. It's this investigation into the theater and everything that's been going on with it."

"It doesn't surprise me in the least. A new building like that going up. In a small town like this. Why, the historical society had so many complaints that first week."

"What does the society do about complaints?" I asked.

"We can bring it up to the planning board meetings that the town holds. And then we contest the decision to bring in the new developer."

"Did you or your society bring up any issues to the planning board?"

"We did. Ilsa Greer was the most upset about the theater going in. Her business is a quiet spa in the evenings, she does most of the client massage work, and if it's loud and busy she said she would lose business. We argued the point with her at the planning board meeting a number of months past."

"What happened?"

"Nothing. The board voted that it wouldn't affect her business enough to offset the number of new jobs it would provide for the town." She folded her napkin.

"I bet she was really angry at that." And then I remembered her perfume.

"You should come to one of the meetings. There's always somebody getting very angry about something."

"I bet." Small towns didn't lack for enthusiasm. "Thanks, Mrs. Orsa. You've cheered me up." I could tell she didn't understand how, but it didn't seem to bother her. I walked back into the kitchen for a bit more privacy in case someone new came into the diner.

I punched in Ellie's cell phone number. "Ellie, can you do me one last favor?"

"Sure, what do you need?"

"Can you take a look at Ilsa Greer? She lives in town so you shouldn't need to hack into anything."

"No problem. I can do it while we're on the phone."

"Thanks." I waited, thinking again about how I was instigating some sort of crime.

"Oh, that's interesting." I could hear typing in the background.

"Looks like she took out a business loan. And she regularly withdraws large sums of cash. I can print this out for you if you'd like."

"No, I don't think that's a good idea. I'll find a way to prove it. Hey, Ellie, thanks!"

"No problem."

I had a new suspect and a motive. As much as I didn't want to do it, Dan had to know.

18

The police station had the air conditioner on low and it was stuffy inside. At the front desk, Officer Jones wasn't happy about it. It was too hot to even bother fighting, so she waved me to the back when I asked to talk to the detective.

"We were going about this all wrong; it wasn't insurance money or stolen cash, it was fear of change. Just like you and Jay can't imagine that Sam has changed.

"Ilsa's business was doing well because it was quiet and calm in the evenings and she had started to finally see profit for her evening couple's retreats that were done outside." Dan wasn't connecting the dots.

"If the theater goes in then the evenings will be filled with people coming and going from the parking lot making a ton of noise and disruption."

"I don't have any evidence that points to Ilsa. But I have evidence that points to Weller."

"It's not Noah Weller. I know from bank statements..." Oops. That was a slip-up.

"Where did you get this information?"

"That doesn't matter."

"It absolutely does matter. You can't be doing this. You got it from Ellie, didn't you? She can get fired for giving you any information. You're toying with people's livelihoods."

"Ellie didn't give me anything." A little lie to save a friend—totally fine.

"I could arrest you."

"Stop throwing that around. I'm helping you, can't you see that?"

"You need to leave before I really do arrest you."

I stormed out of there so fast that by the time I hit the street I still hadn't finished my thought. What was I going to do now?

I took a deep breath. There was one person that could prove that I was right. I had to visit Ilsa Greer.

But first I had to make a detour.

I PARKED near the trailer set up outside the theater. This was where Mr. Weller and Karl had their office. I got out of the car before I could lose my nerve. I climbed the three wooden steps and banged on the door, then I turned the knob and stepped inside.

Noah Weller sat behind a desk staring at paperwork. A stack of folders on his right and a laptop to his left.

"Mr. Weller, I'd like to ask you some questions about the theater." He didn't even look up from his desk.

"I'm sorry, but I am busy with insurance paperwork. I'm swamped. If you have questions maybe I can answer them tomorrow."

"Noah, you have to be my date."

His head shot up at that. "What?" He looked at me incredulously.

"I'm not asking you to donate a kidney. Just be my date and we'll go to the spa and sign up for a couples massage."

"Why?" His mouth hung open.

The easiest thing to do was to tell him everything. "I believe Ilsa Greer is responsible for stealing your sign and for paying off Ron to mess up the construction of the theater all these months. And I'm pretty sure she's the reason he's now dead."

"So, you want me to pretend I'm your boyfriend so we can go into the spa that's owned by a killer?"

"Yes."

"Are you insane?"

"No, this will work."

"We should call the police."

"I already talked to the police, namely Detective Lockheart. He thinks I'm crazy."

"I think I agree with him."

"Look, do you want to find out who's behind all of this crap that has been keeping your theater from opening? She knew that you were near bankruptcy."

Noah fidgeted. I could tell he was keeping something from me. "You're thinking of something. What?"

"Ilsa knew. She and I dated when I first moved out here to supervise the construction of the theater."

"This is all making more sense."

"How do you know she is behind all of this?"

"She didn't want the theater to go in from the very beginning. She petitioned the historical society to vote against anything new coming into the plaza. We don't have much time, if you come with me and pretend to be my date, we can confront Ilsa and we can prove that she was behind all of this, including the murder of Ron Cain."

"I think this is crazy." He stood up from his desk. "But I'm desperate."

"What every girl wants to hear from a date."

"What?" He squinted at me.

"Never mind. Let's go."

19

The first thing I wanted to do was to hit up Ilsa's car. She and Heather always parked in the same spots each day. There could be evidence there. This is what I wanted Detective Lockheart to look into, but I had to see for myself.

I pulled up on the handle and sure enough it was open. I slid in the driver's seat. "What are you doing?" Noah was confused. "I thought we were going to the spa."

"First things first. I want to see if there's any evidence. People always leave stuff in their car and completely forget about it. I'm thinking Ilsa might have done the same." I rummaged the glove box. Nothing. The whole front seat was clean as a whistle.

I popped the trunk.

Noah and I hovered over the trunk as I opened it. Pieces of orange plastic littered the bottom of the compartment.

"That looks like my sign!" Noah yelled.

It was time for us to head into the spa. "Come on let's see if she'll confess."

Ilsa saw us walk in together and forced a smile on her face. "Can I help you?"

Cara was not in the salon. I guessed she had gone home for the night.

"We would like to schedule a couples spa," I said. She looked at me then at Noah. And even as she started to write our names she stopped. "What do you want?"

"Maybe we just want to talk to you about the theater."

"What about the theater?"

"You hated the idea of it coming into the plaza. A spa is meant to be a peaceful place to visit. You were finally making a profit after all these years with your couples' mini retreat behind your spa, the woods back there lending the perfect quiet backdrop for couples to relax for the evening. And people were paying for that privilege too. So, you added more to the set-up. You bought a luxury couch and a hot tub and expanded the hours you opened the back to customers. This was finally pulling your business out of the red. But all of that would go away if a new theater were to bring loud customers to the parking lot at all hours of the evening.

"First you tried to go the legal route to fix this. You went to the historical society and pleaded with them to vote against the idea at the planning board meeting before Noah Weller even showed up."

Surprise registered on Noah's face.

"When that didn't work you were at a loss. You didn't know what to do. Until you met Noah and realized that he was close to broke. It wouldn't take much to push him over the edge and finish this project before it even began.

"You talked to each one of the contractors working on the theater. They all had their faults. It was easy to find Ron and give him a little motivation; he was willing to do whatever you wanted him to do for you. He did everything he could to make the construction take longer. He even encouraged Milo to steal the crane; maybe he even helped. But despite all of his efforts the theater was still going to open.

"Sam was looking forward to the opening, wasn't he? That really made you angry. Angry enough to frame him for stealing the sign. The sign we found pieces of in your car." I held up a piece of the plastic.

"How did you..."

"I opened your car door. It's kind of silly not to lock it, even in a small town like this, especially if you have incriminating evidence inside the trunk."

I flashed back to the night someone graffitied my kitchen. "You were the one who knocked me down the night you ruined my kitchen. Later, you bumped into me on the day Ron's body was found. I remember the smell of gardenias."

"That's Ilsa's perfume." Noah finally joined in.

"Ron threatened to talk. That's why you killed him."

Her face flashed with rage. Noah even took a step back. But it hadn't surprised me. "He opened the water pipe like you discussed but one of the workers was killed. Now there was going to be an investigation. You knew it would lead to Ron, and if Ron got caught you knew he'd sing like karaoke. So, you got rid of him."

"I did. And I'll do the same to you." Her arm flew back and she heaved something. Noah dropped like a stone. One of the black river rocks that Ilsa used for hot stone massage spun in a circle on the linoleum floor.

"You're next." She lunged in my direction. I ran to the back of the spa.

Did she have more stones? Was I about to get one in the back of the head?

I pushed open the back door and ran out into the couple's retreat area. It did look peaceful. But not with a murderer hot on my heels.

My legs churned as I ran into the woods. Maybe I hadn't thought this out thoroughly. Aerie didn't even know I was here. Dan didn't know I was here. No one knew I was here.

My phone rang. I rolled my eyes. Of course, my sister calls now. Of course, she would. Hello mortal danger; Darla calls. You'd think with all her psychic-ness she'd call before I was moments from death.

I was closing on the back of the theater. I pictured Ilsa dragging Ron from the couple's area into the woods, and toward the theater, the same direction I was running. I just had to make sure I didn't become the next body. The sound of her crashing through the underbrush became louder as she got closer and closer behind me. I needed to get to Sam's back door. He always left it open when he was using the pizza oven. That's how Ilsa had planted part of the sign. All the pieces fell into place like a pretty little puzzle in my mind. I just needed to make sure that mind survived this little detour in my planning. I hated when my sister was right.

I had almost made it to Sam's kitchen door. I grabbed the handle. It was locked. Ilsa wrapped her fingers around my neck and squeezed. I kicked backward but she tightened her grip. We fell to the ground. I flashed back to the zigzag marks in the soil where they found Ron's body.

"Stop!" someone shouted. The voice seemed lost in the woods.

My vision tunneled. I frantically pushed at Ilsa's hands,

but all I could manage was to stare into her eyes as her glaring face faded to black. Then suddenly it was over. She was off of me.

I sat up and rubbed at my throat. A moment later, Sam handed me a glass of water. I took a tentative sip. Detective Lockheart had Ilsa cuffed against the back of the building.

"Thanks Sam," Detective Lockheart said.

"No problem. I heard something and when I opened the door, there these two were."

Sam had pulled Ilsa off of me.

"How did you get here so fast?" I asked Detective Lockheart.

"I knew you'd be crazy enough to confront her. I came out here to interview Ilsa to see if any of your claims held water."

"Do you believe me now?"

"Can you try not to get yourself killed?"

"Next time. You were going to say next time." I sucked in air.

"No more next times. I'm tired of saving you from yourself."

"Sam saved me." I looked up with a smile of gratitude at Sam who smiled back.

20

Aerie and I were meeting the boys. When we pulled up in front of the theater you could tell it was a grand opening. Almost the entire town was lined up outside. A big fat red ribbon was draped across the front door. Noah stood there with a big pair of scissors and a smile on his face.

"Quick, hurry up or we will miss it." Aerie had taken much too long deciding which dress to wear to the movies. She said she wanted something new for Sam. They were still super-cute with each other.

We couldn't find the boys, so Aerie and I stood to the side as Noah cut the ribbon. He certainly looked happy. His bank account would look happier after tonight, for sure.

Across the crowd, Ellie stood, grinning wide and holding hands with a tall skinny boy wearing a black T-shirt. She mouthed *This is him*. I guessed that was her secret hacker boyfriend. I secretly hope that they would find a new hobby and stop hacking into forbidden accounts. Or that their relationship would be short-lived. I didn't want to see Ellie get into any trouble. And I decided this investigation would be the last time I would ask her to look up anyone's banking information.

The crowd slowly filed into the theater. It had six screening rooms. I had a good feeling that Noah would do well with this place. We found everyone over by the concessions. Jay and Chelsea were already holding containers of popcorn. Dan ordered, while Sam waved us over.

"The Three Musketeers are back together again," Aerie announced.

"Yeah, I guess we are." Jay said as Chelsea snuggled his arm.

Sam smiled adoringly at Aerie who worked her way around me to hug him.

I felt a little awkward standing there. "Let's go find some seats." Detective Lockheart had just finished ordering his popcorn, and the group of us walked to screening room number two for the latest and greatest movie. Noah had comped us the tickets. He was so happy to have the theater up and running.

Huge reclining armchairs filled the screening room. This was going to be fun.

The six of us found our row of chairs. We all jostled around to organize who would sit where but when we finally dropped into seats, I found myself sitting between Detective Lockheart and Aerie. I glared at Aerie who snuggled into Sam's arm simultaneously elbowing me in mine.

"What?" What was she getting at? She shot a glance over my head. "Detective Lockheart?" I blurted out.

He leaned over in my direction. "You can call me Dan." He offered his container. "Want some popcorn?"

The lights dimmed and the previews started.

"Hey, Mira." Someone crouched in the aisle. When my eyes adjusted, I saw it was Noah. "Thanks again for finding the culprit. I have a present for you. He held up his hands. It took my eyes a moment to focus on two huge clear plastic bags, each holding a ginormous, swimming Koi fish.

"I couldn't afford the upkeep of the tank, so I sold all the pieces off. But Ellie said you loved animals, so I thought I'd give you these as a thank you. I named them, Sign and Crane, after the things that were stolen."

What could I say? "Um, thanks." I took them, one in each hand. What was I going to do with two giant goldfish?

"Enjoy the movie. Thanks again." Noah left me holding the bags, literally.

Cheers erupted as the feature film started.

Dan snickered beside me.

"It wouldn't be so funny if you were the one holding giant goldfish."

"Then, by all means, let me hold one of your giant goldfish."

I handed it to him; his hand brushed mine.

It wasn't terrible, sitting there next to him in the dark. But this wasn't a date. I wasn't dating Dan. Was I?

SNEAK PEEK OF CARNIVALS AND CORPSES

The bright sun of the June afternoon reflected off the chrome detailing on the outside of the Soup and Scoop diner. The iridescent blue of the siding gleamed like car's paint.

Aerie locked the entrance door. We had double-timed the cleanup to get out early. A traveling carnival came to town yesterday, and today was one of the largest openings for the local flea and farmer's market.

Our plan was to take Ozzy, my little terrier, while we shopped at the farmers market for some fresh produce for the diner. While the place was called the Soup and Scoop, the spring and summer months relied heavily on the scoop part, so I was hoping to get some fresh fruit and experiment with new ice cream recipes.

Aerie had mentioned the flea market to me a while back, but this would be my first time attending and I was excited to see what we would find. "Where is this place again?"

"It's where the old drive-in movie theater used to be."

"You forget I didn't not grow up here."

"It's about a mile behind the high school."

I nodded. The town of Pleasant Pond covered a large area full of open acres of land all adjacent to its namesake.

No sooner had I put my seatbelt on than she leaned conspiratorially over to me. "So Mira, what's the deal with you and Dan?" She practically winked.

"Focus on the driving. There's nothing going on between me and Dan."

"Not from where Sam and I were sitting. You guys were getting pretty cozy during the movie last week."

"I don't know what you're talking about. All I remember is some spilled popcorn and when I happened to choke on a kernel, Dan offered me a sip of his soda."

"I knew it! You called him Dan instead of Detective Lockheart." She nodded. "You've got it bad."

I turned my whole body in the seat and stared at her. "You have got to be kidding me. I can't call somebody by their first name without you inferring some deep relationship?"

"Not from you."

"What is that supposed to mean."

"You have been acting weird ever since you met Dan. And I always wondered why." She grinned. "But now I know."

"Know what. Nothing is going on."

"Fight me all you want. The truth is the truth." She was bubbling with laughter. "Well, we're here."

I glanced around surprised. "Really?"

"Yeah, I told you this town is so small everything is next to everything else."

I looked out the window and I could see the ancient drive-in movie screen. It stood like a giant aging white billboard where some brave souls had climbed to the corner and spray-painted graffiti symbols.

On the grounds where cars would normally park for a movie were rows and rows of vendors with prop up tables and gimmicky signs hawking their wares. I couldn't wait. I also desperately wanted to get away from the "Dan" conversation.

I hopped out of the car soon as she set the emergency brake. The summer sun was hot, but a cool breeze blew across the field and fluttered through my T-shirt lifting the sweaty tank top from my back.

The rows of tables in front were set up for the farmer's market. And I already noticed some bright red cherries lying on the closest table. The idea of an almond cherry ice cream popped into my head and I just had to have them. I opened the door to Aerie's back seat and grabbed the reusable shopping bags that she kept there. It was time to go shopping.

Aerie walked around her car with a grin on her face. "You look like a kid in a candy store."

"I feel like one. Do you see those cherries?"

"And I see some strawberries over there. I'm thinking of a vegan strawberry tart." She rubbed her hands together. We made our way over to the tables and the grinning faces of the local farmers. The woman gently packed five pounds of cherries in my bag and glanced up at me, "Another month and we will have honey crisp apples and then after that we'll have more varieties." The idea of apple crisp made my mouth water. "We have pick-your-own starting at the very end of August. Here's our flyer and you can find us online." She added a flyer to my bag and handed one to me.

"Thank you." I took my bag gratefully. Already plotting out the future recipe for the cherry almond ice cream. Maybe I would start boiling down some cherries to make a syrup. I looked around and found Aerie where I expected, near the strawberries the last of the season. "Hey Aerie, I see that farmer Miller has fresh eggs. Would you like to get some for the diner?"

"You're the chef. You know what our customers want." I had only been chef for a couple months. But Aerie enjoyed giving me full rein. "Besides," she said, "I like the idea of supporting Mr. Miller as part of our community."

I took out one of my other shopping bags and shook it open. "Hi, Mr. Miller. Could I ask for about three dozen of your eggs?"

"Buying for the diner?"

"Of course, only the best for our customers." I fumbled trying to open the bag until Mr. Miller offered and opened it for me.

He gently placed three cartons of eggs into my bag, and I paid him probably half what organic eggs cost up north.

"You two should head over to the flea market. My cousin is over there selling some of the antiques he picked up at an auction. He's over there in the blue baseball cap with the dolphin on the front. You just tell him Mike sent you."

"Thanks Mr. Miller." I took the bag of eggs over my shoulder and glanced over at the flea market. It was like a wonderland of random treasures.

"We could put all of this in the car and then browse." Aerie suggested. "I can open up the windows. There is a bit of a breeze. If we're quick, I don't think we have to worry too much."

The weight of three pounds of cherries and three dozen eggs wasn't exceptionally heavy but Ozzy deserved a good walk and I knew if we put it away we could scan through the flea market faster. "Okay let's go."

After putting all of our produce and eggs in the car in the most shaded area we could Aerie rolled down the windows to get some ventilation and we promised it would only be a couple minutes. But I was super excited to check out the flea market.

Ozzy tugged on her leash as Aerie and I wandered down the rows of tables covered in everything from purses and jewelry to antique farming implements. If you were looking for something obscure, I could imagine you could find it here. Along with something as practical as a paring knife. I was still on the hunt for furniture for the house. Anything cheap that was still functional was how I looked at it. Aerie had stopped at a table full of jewelry, bracelets, earrings, necklaces, and beads.

"Isn't this pretty?" She held up a tiny silver teardrop-shaped cage. On closer inspection it held beach glass in different shades of blue and green. "It's gorgeous."

While Aerie paid for her new find I walked further down the aisle noticing a desk that I could definitely put to good use at home. I could already imagine the desk in my living room corner. The seller had an airstream parked behind the table which was full of the odds and ends that you would find in grandma's attic.

As luck would have it it was a man wearing a blue baseball cap with a dolphin on the front, Mike Miller's cousin. He was sweating profusely, and he looked a little preoccupied. I looked over the desk, it appeared to have been recently stained in a warm golden color so the wood shone through a layer of shiny lacquer.

It was an old style rolltop desk and when I pulled down the slatted cover there was a satisfying click as each slat unfolded and connected smoothly with the desktop. I opened it back up and peeked into the tiny drawers on top.

"I'll sell that to you for cheap." Said Mike's cousin. I walked around the desk. It appeared to be in great shape.

"How much you want for it?" I needed to know if this was going to be too rich for my blood. Because pretty much everything was these days.

"How much are you willing to pay?"

"I doubt I have enough for this. It's beautiful."

He nodded curtly. "Name your price."

"40 bucks?" It was all that I had in the pocket of my phone. This antique rolltop desk had to be worth at least 10 times that amount.

"It's yours." He held out his hand and I laid two twenties in his calloused palm. He furtively glanced around and stuffed the 20s in his pocket instead of the lockbox that sat at his table. He saw me glance at it and slammed the box shut, twisted the key and stuffed the key into his pocket.

"I have to go. Enjoy the desk." He ducked through the crowd and I watched as he snatched his hat off his head. And he was lost in the shuffle of people.

Aerie came up behind me "Is that yours?"

I turned back to the desk. "It appears so." I ran a hand along the top of its smooth lacquered surface. "I bought it from Mike Miller's cousin. But he ran off."

"What do you mean he ran off?" A breeze pulled strands of her golden hair from it's elastic.

"He slammed shut his lockbox there, took the key with him and disappeared into the crowd."

"That's odd. Maybe he had to use the facilities." Aerie glanced in the direction of the bathrooms and visibly shivered. She had a thing about outhouses and porta-potties.

"Yeah. Maybe." I looked around his table area. No one else seemed to be with him. I can't imagine anyone leaving their lockbox full of cash unattended, even if they had to use the restroom. He had been acting strangely. I walked behind the table.

Aerie gave me a look. "What are you doing?"

"Something doesn't feel right. He let me buy that desk for next to nothing and he was acting very strange. And then he disappears? Something's up."

"I wish I had seen him maybe his aura would have given us a clue."

The table was covered with a clean yellow tablecloth and a wide selection of antiques. A beat-up wooden music box, a cardboard container of books, random dishes and teacups.

"Ordinary stuff. I don't see anything out of place." Ozzy tugged on her leash as she walked around sniffing the table legs.

Aerie scrutinized the offerings. "No cell phone?"

"I don't see anything." I ducked under the table and noticed a large red and white cooler. I pried up the lid, immediately Ozzy wanted to sample the smells. A zip topped back holding two sandwiches and a six pack of lime soda sat on top of a bed of ice. "Just his lunch." I closed the lid. Ozzy jumped back down and continued to sniff around instead hoping to find a new friend to play with, so I held tight to her leash.

As soon as I stood up Aerie gave me a nod in the direction of the table next to us. "Right." A middle-aged woman completed the sale of a hand-knit ribbed hat. She sat back down picked up her knitting project and continued to knit.

"Excuse me?" I leaned in her direction.

"Can I help you?" She continued to knit even though her eyes were trained on me.

"Do you know the man who sells at this table? Blue baseball cap?"

Her smile was conciliatory. "No, sorry I'm new. This is the first year I'm selling at the flea market."

"You didn't get a chance to talk to him at all?"

"No. I've been a bit busy between sales and my project." She lifted her needles up with the knitted green strands of yarn dangling.

"Okay, thanks." Ozzy was tugging hard on the leash. I looked at Aerie who had walked over to the table across from us. "Any luck?"

"No, she says she didn't know the guy and didn't see anything out of the ordinary."

"We can talk to Mr. Miller; he did mention that this is his cousin."

Aerie put her hand on her hip. "Do you really have that feeling? I mean maybe he just went to the bathroom or had to make a private phone call or something."

I shrugged. I had that gut feeling that tugged at me, but Aerie was right. There was nothing to go on. Ozzy tugged on her leash and whined. "I guess we can go. My spidey sense is just overreacting." I pulled on the leash. "Come on, Ozzy, let's go."

She resisted my tug and whined again. She stood on her hind legs scratching at the wheel well of the airstream trailer parked behind the table. I squatted down to her eye level. "What's up Ozzy? Come on we'll go home and get you some treats?"

And then I smelled what she had scented. Blood. My eyes adjusted to the dark shadow underneath the airstream. That's when I saw the body. I jumped up.

"Well then, I guess we'll be calling Dan." I stood and was practically hyperventilating.

"What? What did you see? Did you have, like a vision?"

"I am not my sister. I do not have visions. There is a body under that airstream."

"Oh my gosh, serious?" It always amazed me how excited Aerie got about anything out of the ordinary. She quickly stepped around the table and went down on her hands and knees to stare into the shadows under the trailer. "Oh boy." She slowly stood and pulled her cell phone out of her back pocket.

"I'll call him."

I nodded agreeing with her because for some reason I always happened to be on the site of whatever new murder happened to occur in our town. And not too long-ago Detective Dan Lockhart had put me in a jail cell for asking too many questions. So, the last thing he needed to see was me at a murder scene.

MORE MIRA MICHAELS MYSTERIES

If you enjoyed this story and would like to read more about Mira and her lovable cat Arnold, check out more of the Mira Michaels Mysteries.

Carnival and Corpses
Pottery and Perps
Gables and Grievances

Please consider writing a review on Amazon to let others know more about Mira's adventures, please don't share spoilers! Reviews help readers find these stories which helps writers like me. That way I can continue to write what I love and create more stories for you.

Thanks bunches,

Julia